A PLOT FOR ANY OCCASION

A CRIME ANTHOLOGY

RUTH M. MCCARTY   SHARON DAYNARD

DONNA RICCI   CAROL KAUFMAN

LAUREN SHERIDAN   RANDALL DEWITT

EDITED BY

KRIS MURPHY AND RANDALL DEWITT

POTTER'S FIELD PUBLISHING

This book is a work of fiction. References to real people, businesses, events, establishments, organizations, or locales are only to provide a sense of authenticity and are used fictitiously. All other characters, incidents and dialog are drawn from the authors' imagination and are not to be considered as real.

ISBN: 978-1-7342454-3-1

Cover Art by Lauren Sheridan

Created with Vellum

For Carol Perry. Our friend, mentor, and partner in crime.

ACKNOWLEDGMENTS

This book wouldn't have been possible without the hard work of the authors who contributed their stories.

FOREWORD

Every day is an occasion. Whether it's a traditional holiday, a designated day of observance, or some kind of appreciation day, they all have one thing in common—crime. Murders, thefts, and any other crimes imaginable, don't take the day off just because it was declared to be special by Congress or by a governor in a statehouse. This book imagines eleven crimes set against the backdrop of both well-known and obscure occasions in our lives.

Ruth M. McCarty kicks off the anthology with a parade in "A Mardi Gras to Remember." Next, Sharon Daynard carves out a story inspired by World Smile Day with her story "Lothario." In "A Matter of Interpretation," Lauren Sheridan translates National Interpreter Appreciation Day into a crime event not to be misunderstood. Randall DeWitt goes to bat for Birthmark Awareness Day in "One Strike Away." Then, Carol Kaufman gives lessons in mahjong tiles and a missing person for National Mahjong Day in her story, "Murder in the Winds." Donna Ricci writes a dissertation about the struggles to make it to National Graduation Tassel Day in her not-so-studious story titled, "Commencing Murder." National Funeral Director and Mortician Recognition Day becomes a conference to miss in DeWitt's story "Bereft of Shame." Sheridan exposes an unhealthy competition between contestants who want to be heard for Town Crier's Day with "A Bellow of Criers." Kaufman returns with more than a shopping experience in "Black Friday Blues." McCarty finds an April Fools' Day snowstorm no laughing matter in "Iced In." And, finally, Daynard does her best to ruin Christmas in "The Most Wonderful Crime of the Year."

We hope you enjoy.

By the way, National Short Story Day has always been the first day of winter. My mind is wandering, wondering what crime would be best suited for the occasion. A writer doing research for a story finding themself a target for murder? Or maybe one who takes their research too far? There are so many possibilities. I can only hope for a sequel, *A Plot for Any Occasion Thickens*, to see how it turns out.

A MARDI GRAS TO REMEMBER

BY RUTH M. MCCARTY

February in Florida can be hot and humid or cold and wet. Doris didn't know which would be worse for the Mardi Gras Golf Cart Parade. Too humid and the crepe paper would wilt. Too wet and the parade would be a disaster.

The *krewe*, the volunteers who were planning the Fat Tuesday parade, had decided to give three prizes this year—Best Theme, The Gaudiest, and The Grand Master, with the couple winning Grand Master named the King and Queen of Carnival.

This was the third year that Doris and Dean had entered. The last two hadn't even brought a mention, honorable or not. All they got were hoots of "Throw me something, mister" as Doris and Dean drove by, tossing foil-wrapped chocolates and strings of beads to the crowds lining the sidewalks.

This year Doris was determined she would win Grand Master. She'd thumbed through online catalogs daily, ordering anything and everything purple, green, and gold, the colors of Mardi Gras. Packages filled the spare bedroom and their golf cart had been spit-shine cleaned, with only one day left before the parade.

"This isn't the Macy's Day Parade," Dean said, eying the

boxes piling up. "You're spending more on this than the top prize money."

Doris gave him a side-eyed glare. He just didn't understand the hierarchy at the clubhouse. Elise Peyton had won the coveted Grand Master prize for the last eight years. She was the president of the garden club, a top golfer and tennis player. Tan and thin. And she was nice. Everyone loved Elise.

Doris wanted to just once have people remember her name. Remember that she'd joined the ladies club. Volunteered at all the parties. She'd smiled and said hello to the ladies at the pool, at the spa, and on the courts.

Well, this year they'd remember her name. Or else.

ON FRIDAY MORNING, Doris went about setting out the decorations. Not only for the golf cart, but for her and Dean, too. She would be Queen of Carnival and Dean would be her King.

After endlessly researching what the Mardi Gras colors stood for, she'd bought a purple gown from an online store that specialized in Celtic and Renaissance styles. A gauzy, maxi dress, with flowing sleeves worthy of royalty. Purple because it's the color of Justice and fit for a queen. She would finally get her due.

Dean would wear gold for Power. He'd insisted on wearing shorts, so she'd found him a glitzy pair with sparkly boat shoes to match, along with a colorful Mardi Gras vest and bow tie to jazz him up.

She'd bought a purple and gold masquerade mask for herself with a purple feather that curled in a semicircle. Dean's mask was green and gold and shaped like a crown—reminding her of the masquerade balls in Regency London in her beloved romance novels.

Green represented Faith, and she had plenty of that. Faith that now that she'd come up with a plan. She would finally reign.

On Saturday morning she and Dean were up at dawn. The day was glorious! Low in the seventies with a minimal breeze. The parade would start at five-thirty that afternoon, travel around the complex, stop at the judges table, and end at the clubhouse at six. The judges would have made their picks and the prizes would be announced as the sun set behind them.

Those who had bought tickets would then go inside for dinner and dancing. Because of the COVID-19 pandemic, the committee had to have the dinner catered this year. No one could bring in food and the caterers were going to serve everyone to avoid contamination. The condo association was strict about the rules. They would, however, allow the members to bring their own drinks.

Doris had volunteered to make the famed Mardi Gras Hurricane Punch and the *krewe* had thought it a brilliant idea. She'd donated all the ingredients. Maybe they'd remember her now. Half part overproof rum, one part dark rum, one part light rum and passion fruit to give it a nice red color. She'd bought plastic hurricane glasses at one of the dollar stores in town and had ordered Mardi Gras drink umbrellas. And she'd bought bottles of maraschino cherries that she'd soak overnight in her special Mardi Gras marinade.

She and Dean had brought all of it, except the cherries, to the clubhouse the night before and locked them in the community kitchen. The caterer would open the bottles and mix the punch, making sure the pandemic rules were followed. Doris would have to decide whether she would sneak the marinated cherries inside.

Trembling with excitement, Doris pictured the sun setting behind her as she received her trophy and check. Not that she wanted the money. She only wanted the fame. And the crown. She and Dean would finally be crowned King and Queen of Carnival.

"Honey?" Dean drew her out of her daydream. "Hold this end so I can tape it."

They spent the morning skirting the cart in shiny metallic fringe before adding on layers of decorations with double-sided tape. Masks, metallic streamers, garlands with jesters, cardboard masquerade monsieur and mademoiselle silhouettes cropped to appear as passengers in the back seat. Foil table bursts were stuck in every open space. No part of the golf cart was visible. All that was left was the massive number of helium balloons in the Mardi Gras colors that Dean would pick up later in the day and tape to the roof of the cart.

Doris stepped back and clasped her hands together. "It's perfect, Dean," she whispered. "There's no way I won't win."

~

Doris felt like she was parading in London. The masses lined the streets. Yelling, waving to her. She threw foil-covered chocolates and purple, green and gold beads from the jazz blaring cart. Doris loved it. She gave her best royal wave. A big-bellied man ran in front of them calling "Throw me something, sister" as he pulled up his shirt and the crowd roared.

As they rounded the corner, the judges table came into sight. Each golf cart stopped in front of it. Throwing goodies to the judges, blowing kisses and much pretending of baring breasts took place. Doris watched as Elise Peyton and her husband stopped.

Doris could never remember his name.

Her heart swelled as she saw how plain their golf cart was. Real flowers. Like the centerpieces for the tables! What was Elise thinking? A Rose Parade float? Garden show exhibit? They were wilting already.

Doris shivered in anticipation. She would win for sure.

She and Dean stopped at the table. She tossed beads with plastic shot glasses attached. The judges smiled and clapped. Wrote on their sheets.

Parking spaces were reserved for the carts. They pulled up next to each other. The air was thick with anticipation.

A professional photographer snapped photos. Even the local cable news station was there. Doris grinned, her chest swelling with pride. The judges appeared. The crowd quieted.

Tom Langton, the president of the club, held a microphone. On the table behind him were three trophies and the coveted crowns.

"Ladies and Gentlemen." Tom swept his arms toward the crowd. "I know I say this every year, but I think this year's carts are the best. I wish we could give a prize to all who entered. But, alas, we can't. The judges have tallied their scores and have chosen the winners. When I call your name, please come up and receive your prize and please stay up here for photos."

Doris took several breaths. If they didn't get to it soon, she would surely pass out.

Would Elise's pathetic entry even make the cut this year?

Tom Langton continued, "We are going to start with the prize we think is the most fun. And it looks like you all had fun with this category."

"Come on, get on with it," Doris mumbled under her breath. This was her moment.

"And the prize for The Gaudiest goes to Doris and Dean Davis."

The crowd roared. Doris's face burned. She couldn't move. Dean had to yank her arm to pull her up to the judges. "Smile," he said, out of the corner of his mouth.

Tom handed Dean the envelope and Doris the trophy. The other judges placed jester hats on their heads. Lights flashed from cameras as the sun set behind her.

Doris stared at the grinning faces. She didn't hear the rest of the ceremony. Didn't hear that Elise took Grand Master for the ninth year in a row.

All she could think about was the cherries she'd been marinating in the antifreeze that Dean had saved from the cold New England winters and the RV they'd left behind. The nice red color and sweet taste would be perfect to add to the Hurricane Punch. Just enough to make everyone feel ghastly.

She reached into her bag and touched the cool glass jar, reassured it was still there. She smiled at the crowd as the photographer captured the moment.

Mardi Gras is celebrated the day before Ash Wednesday.

LOTHARIO

BY SHARON DAYNARD

A familiar chill crept down Jane Kline's spine as she waded thigh-high through scarlet waves of flowering bee balm plants along the wrought iron fence of the Victorian where she rented a room. He was watching. Again.

Any other morning, a neatly folded newspaper would have been on the front porch waiting for her to scoop up and whisk into the kitchen to be presented to her elderly landlady. Not that Mrs. McGilroy cared about editorials, political commentaries or sports. She used those pages to line her bird's cage. The murders were the real news. Boston could keep its decades-old stories of the Strangler and his thirteen victims. Portsmouth had the Lothario and he was just getting started.

The city was buzzing with the gruesome homicides and Mrs. McGilroy loved it. Neighbors she hadn't seen in years, people she didn't even know were still alive, were dropping by and sitting on her porch to gab about them. Even the priests at Saint Jerome's made a point of mentioning the victims in their sermons and offering up a special prayer. They didn't go into any of the grisly details, much to Mrs. McGilroy's disappointment, but hoped their suffering had been brief and each had found the comfort of faith in their final moments.

Six months ago, the first murder barely managed four lines

in the Crime & Courts section of the *Portsmouth Ledger.* Tina Marie Millman and the red lipstick smile smeared across her face were buried among the break-ins, aggravated assaults and DWIs. Even if the killer had a sense of humor, a working girl turning up dead wasn't front page news.

Number 2 made the front page, but that was pretty much a given when the mayor's ex-wife turned up dead. Like Tina Marie Millman, Suzanne Webster's throat was slashed from ear to ear with the same pathetic lipstick grin painted across her face. It was only after Number 3, Willie Dobbs, that the police figured out they had a psychopath on their hands. It was in the Dobbs write-up that the *Ledger* dubbed the killer the Lothario.

The *NY Times* and *CNN* picked up the story after Number 3, joining in with everyone and their brother to formulate a scenario that linked the victims together. Tina Marie Millman, 42, was last seen working her usual corner. Suzanne Webster 43, never made it home after attending a moonlight performance of *The Tempest* in Prescott Park. Willie Dobbs, 30, missed the 7 PM registration cutoff at the Good Shepherd Shelter. Tina Marie was found in one of the city's seedier motels, having paid cash for the room on a one-hour rental. Suzanne turned up in her abandoned car and Willie in the Piscataqua River.

Numbers 4 and 5 threw everyone for a loop. Twenty-six-year-old identical twins, Darla and Delia Newsome, were found in the storeroom of Two Scoops, their downtown ice cream parlor. Their throats were slashed inches below the telltale smiles. Apparently having run out of Kiss-Me-Red lipstick, the Lothario took to capping the twins' teeth with maraschino cherries.

Number 6 hadn't been more than a week ago. Jeff Cleary, a thirty-eight-year-old RN, husband and father of three, working the graveyard shift at the Water's Edge Nursing Home was murdered in the facility's laundry room. Coworkers and residents never heard so much as a whimper as Cleary's throat was ripped out and a pair of 5-inch stainless steel laundry pins fastened his mouth into a morbid grin.

"Janey!" Mrs. McGilroy's shrill voice permeated Jane's skull like nails on a chalkboard. "How long does it take to bring in the paper!"

God forbid Mrs. McGilroy joined the rest of the world and subscribed to cable and internet services for the news.

"Coming!" Jane dropped on hands and knees and scanned the shrubs at ground level. On those rare occasions when the paperboy's aim was less than accurate, the newspaper landed on the porch steps or walkway. This morning, it was nowhere to be found. There were only two explanations, either it hadn't been delivered or it had been stolen. Again. To the *Ledger*'s credit, the only day that subscribers hadn't received their morning newspaper was November 10, 1965—the morning after the Great Blackout.

Last night, the lights hadn't so much as flickered.

In the eight months since Everett Kent purchased the house across the street and hung out his Seacoast Smiles shingle, Mrs. McGilroy's paper had magically appeared on the oral surgeon's doorstep too many times to be considered accidental. On each occasion, Kent waited until Jane made an exhaustive search before he wandered across the street with his yappy Yorkie, Ophelia, and the stray paper along with what Jane assumed was a witty apology. Each time, he extended an offer to properly introduce himself over cocktails, following up the proposition with a dazzling, disarming smile and a wink, as if intimating what cocktails might lead to. And each time, Jane snatched the paper from his hand and retreated into the Victorian without comment. Despite her landlady's assertion, the last thing Jane Kline needed was a man in her life. She'd tried them before and wasn't impressed.

What little Jane knew of Everett Kent was overheard in the whispered conversations of the women she worked with at the library and from the secondhand stories Mrs. McGilroy brought home from the beauty parlor and bingo night at the senior center. Depending on who Jane listened to, Kent's marital status ran the gamut from confirmed bachelor, recently divorced, to tragically widowed. He was a perfect gentleman, a ladies' man or the devil himself. He was from London, Liverpool or Leeds. He was a hobnobber, a philanthropist and patron of the arts, a connoisseur of fine wines, aged whiskies and two-for-one draft nights. The only thing Jane knew with any degree of certainty was Everett Kent had become a local celebrity. There wasn't a man who didn't want to be him or woman who didn't want to be with him.

Against her better judgement, Jane looked across the street and saw Everett Kent watching from his front window. Pretending not to have noticed him, she continued her search pushing aside the dense clusters of Autumn Joy Sedum and black-eyed Susans that camouflaged the deteriorating lattice work at the base of the Victorian's wraparound porch. And there it was, perfectly wedged inside one of the broken lattice cells, just waiting for someone to offer a helpful hand and find it. Desperate to be out of Kent's sight, Jane grabbed the paper, rushed up the porch stairs and retreated into the foyer with the early-edition of the *Ledger*.

~

MRS. MCGILROY TOOK in a deep breath and held it as she unfolded the paper, mindful not to crimp or tear the pages. A gasp escaped her lips as she scanned the headline.

"Another one!" She looked from the paper to Jane. "That makes seven. A young man this time."

She ignored Jane's sigh. It hadn't gone unnoticed that any matchmaking attempts on her part to find Jane a husband had taken a backseat to the Lothario over the last six months.

"God bless 'em," Mrs. McGilroy marveled. "They've already notified the next of kin and got hold of a photograph. Pre-debauchery of course!"

As if on cue, the shrill squeal of the teakettle ricocheted through the kitchen. Eyes glued to the lead story, Mrs. McGilroy wandered across the kitchen, pulled the kettle from the burner and filled a mug with boiling water. One hand fumbled through the cabinet, pushing past cans of this and boxes of that before coming to rest on a jar of Folgers. Holding the paper in one hand, she wedged the jar under her armpit, unscrewed the lid with her free hand and shook instant coffee into the mug.

Her eyes darted from the print to the photograph and back as she made her way across the cigarette-scarred linoleum floor, undaunted by the more than a bit of coffee that sloshed out. She settled back into her chair at the breakfast table, mesmerized by what she deemed Pulitzer material. Savoring every word, she mouthed the opening paragraphs. Nose crinkled and shoulders hunched, she delighted in the reporter's command of descriptive adjectives.

"Oh, he's good," she applauded. "'A blood-soaked Rorschach oozed through the crisp white linen covering the corpse.' Now tell me that ain't journalism!"

"It sounds like an excerpt from a cheesy crime novel," Jane said.

Mrs. McGilroy snapped the paper to attention. "Teddy Braver. Twenty-five and single," she passed the news along to Jane.

Single, married, divorced or widowed, they all met the same end.

"Graduated from the University of New Hampshire with a Bachelor's Degree in Art History. Assistant branch manager at Harbor Bank."

Not that occupation played a key role.

"Art history?" Mrs. McGilroy's face twisted into a knot. "Considering the cost of a college education, that's an awful frivolous waste of four years. What kind of a future is there for a young man in art history? Apparently, not much."

Chastising herself for the callous quip, she pulled a yellow marker from her housecoat and began highlighting whatever information she deemed noteworthy.

"The smile was carved out like a jack-o'-lantern! Dear Lord, that must have stung." Mrs. McGilroy looked back to the photograph, trying to picture a zigzagging happy face chiseled into Number 7's striking features. She pressed the capped end of the marker to her temple and traced several jagged patterns along her jaw, each more exaggerated than its predecessor.

"Poor thing." She smirked, making a mental note to light a candle for Number 7 at mass. It was the least she could do.

Her smirk unfurled into a full-blown smile as she turned to the next page. The *Ledger* had devoted the entire third page to the Lothario, recapping each of the previous six murders. Tapping the highlighter against the edge of the table, she prayed it didn't go dry before she was done.

At eighty-three, there wasn't much that sparked an interest in her, but the Lothario lit a flame. Portsmouth had itself a bona fide serial killer without as much as a single clue. No one saw anyone coming or going. Nobody heard any screams

"Poor Teddy Braver. He didn't live more than three blocks away. Engaged to be married next weekend," she muttered to Jane. "They'll never get the deposit back on the hall with this short a notice."

"Getting a deposit back is probably the last thing on his fiancée's mind."

"If you want coffee, Janey, we're out of milk. You'll have to improvise. Try adding a spoonful of that frozen custard I spent a fortune for. From what I hear, it's how Dr. Kent takes his coffee."

Rolling her eyes, Jane opted for juice.

"I tried something different with my hair. I watched a Bette Davis retrospective at the film festival last night. I tried to copy one of her hair styles from *All About Eve*. What do you think?"

Reluctantly, Mrs. McGilroy looked up from the paper as Jane twirled in a full circle before taking a seat.

"Do you like it?"

Raising an eyebrow at the rat's nest hanging from the nape of Jane's neck, Mrs. McGilroy cast the paper aside.

"Why don't you drink your juice and I'll see what I can do." Reaching into the pocket of her housecoat, she felt around for a hairbrush.

"Looks like the neighborhood stray hacked up a furball on the back of your head," she said, tugging on the jumble of hair, bobby pins and hair spray. "You might as well read about Number 7. I could be here until midnight trying to work this mess into something presentable."

With a nod, Jane reached across the table for the paper.

"Don't you just love that word *heinous*?" Mrs. McGilroy tapped the opening paragraph with the brush. "It just sets the mood for the whole story. Now nefarious, that's another good one, but it doesn't quite roll off your tongue the same as heinous. Odious, on the other hand, sounds just plain snotty."

Jane shrugged. Neither heinous nor nefarious were part of her everyday vocabulary. Nasty, ugly words always made Mrs. McGilroy smile.

"Handsome, wasn't he?" Mrs. McGilroy asked.

Jane nodded, glancing from the article to the photograph.

"Reminds me of a young Gregory Peck. Now there's a man that aged well. You wouldn't catch me complaining if he'd left cracker crumbs in my bed. Poor Number 7, he had everything to live for. Just starting out and about to tie the knot."

Jane nodded again.

"Does he look familiar?"

Jane shrugged and turned the page.

"You don't suppose he's the one that called me from the bank with his panties all in a wad accusing me of… What did he call it? Kiting? Imagine someone accusing an eighty-three-year-old widowed saint of something that sounds downright felonious."

"It was probably the manager that called," Jane said.

Mrs. McGilroy made a sour face and muttered something Jane couldn't quite make out. Whatever it was sent a wave of absolute giddiness through the old woman.

Hunching her shoulders and scrunching her nose, Mrs. McGilroy let out an impish giggle. "Just thinking 'bout it gets me weepy, Janey, but enough about delicate old ladies being verbally manhandled. It's you I'm worried about. It's not safe for a little thing like you to be all alone. I couldn't bear the thought of something happening to you. It's hard enough running a boarding house with one tenant let alone none. I'd have to close the McGilroy Arms."

"McGilroy Arms?" Jane turned away from the story to look up at her landlady.

"I worry about you, Janey. You need a man. A man like Dr. Kent. He'd be quite the catch. He's English."

"So was Jack the Ripper." Jane turned back to the front-page photo of Teddy Braver.

"Always finding fault, aren't you, Janey?"

"Did you know surgeon is fifth on the Top Ten List of Occupations for Psychopaths?" Jane asked. "Isn't Dr. Kent an oral surgeon?"

"Stop trying to change the subject. One man leaves you standing at the alter and you give up on love."

"It wasn't one man."

"Excuse, me. One at the altar, another left you high and dry at the Motel 6 and your prom date ditched you. Do I have to go all the way back to the paste-eater in kindergarten that broke your heart?" She stepped back, looked at Jane's hair and sighed.

"Your hair's just too fine for that kind of updo. Women had a lot more hair back in the fifties. We didn't need fancy gels and foams. A trip to the beauty parlor once a week for a wash and set, a can of hair spray and a good sleeping bonnet was all we needed. None of that foolish scrubbing your scalp raw every day in the shower. You're better off with a ponytail, dear."

She combed Jane's shoulder length, flyaway hair from her face. "Hair this baby-fine should be bobbed into a pixie or pageboy, something that frames your face. A good perm couldn't hurt. Even pin curls would be an improvement."

"Yes, Mrs. McGilroy."

"What you need is a perm *and* a man. You've got to get out more, Janey. You spend too much time at that job and going to school. What kind of a life is that, working at a library? What kind of man are you going to find there? I've seen the men that use the library. Perverts with comb-overs and clammy palms. Men too cheap to buy a book. What you need is a job in a bookstore. Professional men buy books."

"Dr. Kent has a library card. He borrows three to four books every week and he joined the Jane Austen Book Club. He mentors students prepping for their SATs and—"

"Reads to shut-ins and the infirmed. Dr. Kent's not the one who's hard up for a date. You are. Spend a little more time on yourself instead of all that foolish volunteer work. If you want to volunteer your time, do it at a hospital. Doctors make fine husbands. Just don't get roped into signing one of those prenups. When you finally land a man like Dr. Kent, you'd best make certain you're into him for all he's worth." Mrs. McGilroy twisted an elastic about Jane's hair and sat back down across from her.

"Doll yourself up a bit, Janey. A little rouge and mascara. I've been around long enough to know what a man wants and believe me, it's not Susie Homemaker. Not unless she's got a G-string and garters under that apron."

Jane's head shot up from the paper.

"Wake up, Janey. You're thirty-six and counting. It's not likely you're going to attract a man with that degree of yours. Show a little cleavage. A bit of thigh. A preview of coming attractions. That's how you'll land a man."

"Thank you for the advice, Mrs. McGilroy, but I'm perfectly happy with my life just the way it is."

"How? It's not natural. A woman needs a man. It's what the bible says."

"I don't recall 'Thou shalt not stay single' being one of the Ten Commandments. I doubt I'll burn in hell if I go to my grave a single woman."

"The word's spinster. You'd be doing yourself a favor taking a few lessons from me. I could teach you a trick or twenty. I was quite the looker in my day."

Mrs. McGilroy planted her hands on her massive hips, swayed her shoulders from side to side, tilted her head back and smiled. Her yellowed teeth were all the more exaggerated by the garish lipstick she insisted gave new definition to the word voluptuous. Lipstick so red, it made her dentures look as if they'd been soaked overnight in urine. "I could've had any man I wanted back then."

"I'm sure you could."

"I knew what it took to put a smile on a man's face. They couldn't resist me. They all want a buxom woman. Don't let those women's libbers tell you otherwise. The bigger the better."

Jane made a face and looked back to the paper.

"You know, Janey, a bit of padding in that department couldn't hurt. I'm not saying you should run out and get one of those boob jobs, but a few strategically placed tissues might turn your love life around. What about one of those computer-engineered brassieres or some of those silicon cutlets? Breast enhancers, they call them. Guaranteed to lift and smoosh absolutely nothing into an impressive cleavage."

"I'm quite capable of finding a man without the benefits of mascara, tissues and the marvels of modern technology."

"Really? And how do you propose to do that? Dazzle 'em with the Dewey Decimal System? What happened to that nice Steven what's-his-name? You know, the one that actually made a repeat performance."

"Things didn't work out." Jane flipped to the Arts and Entertainment section of the paper. "He moved on to bigger and better things."

"As I recall, she was a 36D and blonde."

"She was a bimbo."

"One woman's bimbo is another man's Aphrodite."

"I'm sure that's very profound on some level, but if I don't hurry, I'll miss my bus." Grabbing a brown paper bag from the table, Jane shoved it into her canvas tote and hurried for the door.

"Be careful and keep your eyes out for a man, Janey! There's gotta be one out there for you. A nice fella with dark glasses and a guide dog, maybe."

"WELL, if it isn't the late Jane Kline." Ruth Quimby sneered. "Tardy as usual."

"It wasn't my fault."

"It never is."

"The bus driver didn't see me—"

"At the stop, again," Ruth finished her sentence. "If you're going to make up an excuse, at least put a little thought into it. The bus careened down a ravine and burst into flames. Mrs. McGilroy finally took that stroke she's been promising everyone. You were having tea with the Lothario and lost track of time."

"It won't happen again." Jane found it almost impossible to keep her voice from cracking. She wasn't going to cry, not in front of Ruth Quimby. It'd only give her another excuse to lecture. Hanging her head, Jane hurried into the break room, tossed her lunch into the fridge and made a quick dash to the ladies' room.

Looking into the full-length mirror, she pushed her bangs from her eyes and frowned. Mrs. McGilroy was right, her hair was awful.

Straightening her skirt and blouse, she pouted. She hated the olive drabs and tans that overwhelmed her wardrobe. This morning, she must have felt on the cutting edge, going out on a limb with a sage-green skirt and matching top.

She shrugged, surveying her figure. She had an all right body. She was tall, maybe a bit too tall, and slender. Some might say thin, but she was nowhere close to emaciated like Mrs. McGilroy insisted.

Maybe if she wore her skirts a little shorter, she'd turn a few heads. Gathering up the surplus of material, she revealed a pair of shapely calves in sheer black hose. Not bad, she thought. Maybe instead of lunch she'd do some shopping, upgrade her wardrobe, live a little.

"Jane Kline, are you in there? I want that bulletin board for the fall reading series finished today! It's your turn for shelving and cleaning the fish tank you insisted the reading room needed. Is that understood?" Ruth rapped the door for emphasis and walked away.

"Yes, ma'am."

For close to three hours Jane worked on the display of autumn leaves falling from a tree. She'd spent most of the week photocopying book covers, cutting them into leaves and tinting them with red, orange and yellow watercolors. Above the scene, bright orange letters spelled out LEAF THROUGH A GREAT BOOK.

Returning her ruler, stapler gun and scissors to her tote, she stood back, looked at the display and groaned. It was even more nauseating than it sounded when Ruth suggested it. Looking up at the clock, she winced. She still had a good five hours to go before packing up and heading home for another adventure packed evening with Mrs. McGilroy and the Lothario.

A CHILLING RAIN started falling shortly after Jane returned from lunch and hadn't let up. In her early morning exodus, she hadn't thought to grab an umbrella or jacket. The evening edition of the *Ledger* would have to serve as the only protection her head had from the rain. She couldn't care less about the latest insights on the Lothario. Mrs. McGilroy would fill her in on any gruesome details that might have surfaced over the last few hours.

Jane glanced down at her watch and then up the street. The bus was fifteen minutes late. The handful of people that started out at the stop with her had all either found rides, flagged down cabs or called an Uber. She was alone.

A steady stream of water poured off the paper and down the front of her, soaking her shoes. Drivers splashed her as they sped past in a hurry to get somewhere warm and dry. Her wet blouse clung to her skin giving her goosebumps.

A smile spread across her face as a set of headlights approached. As the bus got closer, she stepped to the curb and waited for it to slow to a crawl before opening its doors. In disbelief she watched as it came and went without so much as a beep.

The next bus wasn't due for another hour. A cab was out of the question. She never carried more than five dollars in her wallet. She didn't have an Uber account. The best she could do was slip inside somewhere dry and wait. Returning to the library wasn't even worth debating. She could just picture Ruth cackling when she heard that yet another bus driver hadn't seen her. The only nearby place to get out of the rain for a while was The Last Call.

Mustering her courage, Jane walked up to the bar's front door. The smell of cheap perfume and stale beer assaulted her before she even stepped inside. It took a few minutes for her eyes to adjust to the dim lighting. Looking around, she wished they hadn't. Mrs. McGilroy would have called it ambiance, but even the word "sleazy" didn't do its squalor justice. Poster-sized ads insinuating a direct correlation between alcohol consumption and an ardent love life masked the stained wallpaper. Peanut shells and cocktail napkins littered the floor, soaking up the spilled drinks.

Laundered table linens and a ventilation system were apparently a luxury the management felt they could do without. What sounded like music infused with shrieking bagpipes blared over the rough language and less than discreet conversations. A couple of waitresses, preferring their cleavages over apron pockets for holding cash, strutted about the tables. All the place needed were flames shooting up from the floor to convince Jane that she'd stumbled into Happy Hour in Hell.

She noticed a man staring at her. With his clipper cut, light brown hair and chiseled jawline, he reminded her of the actor Scott Eastwood. She looked away, afraid he'd mistake her gaze for an invitation and approach. Then she thought of Mrs. McGilroy and her dissertations on men and the fine art of vamping. Wouldn't Mrs. McGilroy just die if she showed up for dinner with Scott's better-looking brother?

Jane straightened her skirt, smiled and looked him directly in the eye. Mrs. McGilroy insisted eye contact was crucial. His were the bluest eyes she'd ever seen. He was perfect and he was still looking at her. Blushing, she tossed back her wet mane of hair. According to Mrs. McGilroy, body language said everything.

Returning her smile, he winked.

She watched in awe as he crossed the room. As he got closer, his perfect smile broadened, exposing an expanse of blinding white teeth. She swore she could make out the scent of Burberry cologne through the bar stench.

And like the bus, he kept moving on to whatever stop lay beyond her.

No problem. He wasn't her type anyway. At least Mrs. McGilroy wasn't there to critique her obvious shortcomings when it came to mating rituals. All she had to do was get through the next few minutes and she'd be fine. A cocktail would help pass the time, make her look like she was part of the crowd. Walking up to the bar, she pulled the five-dollar bill from her wallet and waived it in the air. "Excuse me. A tonic water and lime, please."

The bartender moved on to the next customer and filled his order.

"Excuse me."

Again, the bartender looked passed her.

Gritting her teeth, she shoved the money back into her purse and looked about the crowded room. Her stomach clinched when she saw a face she recognized at the far end of the bar. He excused himself from the enamored women seated on either side of him and headed toward her. Unlike the bus and Scott Eastwood's better-looking brother, Dr. Everett Kent stopped and asked if he could buy her a cocktail.

She wanted to say yes. She wanted to let loose and enjoy herself for a change. Instead, she panicked. She shook her head and darted out the door.

"Ms. Kline!" Kent called out, rushing to catch up with her

in the parking lot. "I didn't mean to offend you. Truly, I didn't. I just thought…" His voice trailed off noticing the way her wet clothes clung to her body.

"I'm not the bar type," she tried to explain. "I missed the bus and it was raining—"

"Completely understandable, Ms. Kline. A hot cup of coffee and a lift home then?" He smiled as a gust of wind caught the hem of her skirt, revealing French lace garters and sheer black stockings.

~

"I've always had a fondness for naughty librarians, Ms. Kline. Do you mind if I call you, Jane? I'm betting you've read every book in the adult section, haven't you, Jane?" Everett Kent leered, edging her skirt up her thighs.

"We don't stock pornography." Jane squirmed away and looked out the window. A knot tightened in her stomach and tears welled up in her eyes realizing she'd made a terrible mistake getting in his car.

"Tell me, is it true you can't judge a book by its cover?" He pulled her closer as he turned the car in to a motel parking lot. "I bet you come here all the time, don't you?"

"No. No, I don't." She shrank away. "I thought we were going for coffee."

"Surely, you've heard of room service, Jane?" He pulled the car into a space at the back of the building. "I know all about teases like you. You're not the goody-goody everyone thinks you are." He leaned across the seat, pressing her back up against the car door.

"Please, I just want to go home." Her eyes frantically searched the vacant parking lot.

"Home? The fun's just starting." He grinned, unbuttoning her blouse.

"Stop it!" She squirmed, trying to shift his weight from her.

"Well, what do we have here?" he asked as her blouse fell

about her waist revealing a black lace bustier. "No sense wasting good money on a room when we're warm and cozy right here."

"No!" She shoved him back.

He searched her tear-streaked face, grabbed a fistful of hair and snapped her head back. "You had me going there for a minute, Jane. You like playing games, don't you?"

Tears streamed down Jane's cheeks. She shook her head. Groping for the door handle, one hand found the tote, the other attempted to fend off his attack.

"Please," she sobbed.

"You don't have to beg for it. Come on, Jane, give us a cheeky smile. I'm all yours." She winced as he pulled harder, pinning her head back against the window. "You like it rough, don't you?"

Her eyes opened wide as the glint of the razor sliced through the air. Blood splattered her face and chest as bloodied hands pawed in disbelief at the gaping wound and the gurgled sound of breathless screams filled the car.

"You'll never know how rough." She sneered, watching the last few convulsive jerks of his body. "That frown will never do."

Looking back on her handiwork, she smiled returning the staple gun to her tote. "Mrs. McGilroy isn't the only one who knows how to put a smile on someone's face."

World Smile Day is celebrated around the globe on the first Friday of October.

A MATTER OF INTERPRETATION

BY LAUREN SHERIDAN

I had repeated the lie so often, I almost believed it myself. Almost. The words tumbled out by rote. I could hear myself saying them in a sober tone tinged with gratitude. *It was quite peaceful in the end.*

I would pause, which was universally received with a gentle nodding of the head, an embarrassed relief betraying itself as a mourning smile that shouted its grief in equal measure with a hearty note of self-congratulations at landing the role of mourner rather than mourned.

Yes, quite comfortable. We said our good-byes. She received the last rites and slipped away.

For good measure, I added a sad but reassuring half-smile to really sell it. Though admittedly, it was not a difficult sale to make. After all, like all good con-artists, I simply told the mark what he or she desperately wanted to hear.

The words of Iago rang in my ears: *How am I a villain?*

My high heels echoed through the deserted courtyard, ringing off the quadrangle of buildings until it filled the whole of the space. The reverberating *click, click* hypnotized me, and my mind drifted, drawn to the question of whether or not the true mark of the best con-artist, wasn't themselves. If they could believe, they could make others believe. After all, so much in life is a matter of interpretation.

In that moment, the scent of lavender assailed me, and my gorge rose. I scurried to the herbaceous border, leaning over, inadvertently, bringing myself closer to the noxious scent. My hand flung to my mouth. It was only then, I remembered my mask, my second face. The simple act of touching the mask provided the distraction that brought me back from the edge, to myself. My stomach settled, though my breaths remained short and shallow. It was, after all, just a scent, and one that I had once loved. But that had changed this summer, along with so many other things.

Taking a step back, I collided into a solid figure.

"Geez, will you watch where you're going, lady!"

I mumbled a reflexive *sorry* to the receding back of a stout man striding past me toward the entrance to West Hall. His stride lengthened to ensure his position at the head of his phalanx of followers, who trooped behind him, jockeying for position near the "great man." None of whom gave me a second glance.

I stood irresolute at the side of the path. My skin prickled in an anaphylactic reaction to my indecision. To calm myself, I activated the relaxation mode on my smartwatch and followed the animated flower that blossomed, dropped its petals, and was reborn—a phoenix rising from the ashes. I timed my breaths. IN *one-two-three*, OUT *one-two-three.* With each breath, the scent of lavender surrounded any lingering doubts like white blood cells engulfing an invading virus, breaking down its defenses and eating away at it, bit by bit, until it vanished without a trace.

Minutes later, I pushed open a heavy, oak door. A gilt plaque proclaimed it to be the Finch Room. The key players milled around a large oak table in the darkly paneled function room. Some wore masks, others did not. None of them maintained the mandatory six-foot social distance.

As I walked in, a blinding light rendered me senseless for a moment. It disoriented me until I realized that someone had turned on a Klieg light.

"Jesus H. Christ. What the hell do you think you are doing, you moron?" bellowed Dick Bragg, the man who had just collided with me a few moments earlier.

A blush suffused the pale skin of a twenty-something deer-in-the-headlights. The young man turned off the light, plunging the room into a temporary darkness until our eyes adjusted to the ambient light once more.

"I was trying to… take a lighting check," he stammered.

Bragg puffed out his chest, smirked, and shook his head.

"Give us a bit of a warning, next time. Jeez." He relaxed the smirk into a smile infused with warmth. "Don't worry about it, kid. We love ya."

Charmed and relieved, the young man turned back to the array of camera equipment in front of him and conferred with a colleague.

Erin Howe slipped one arm under Bragg's and placed the other carefully manicured hand on his sleeve, leaning in so that his arm nestled between her ample breasts before skillfully maneuvering him away from the lighting setup toward me. As they moved closer, I heard Bragg say in a low voice, "Get rid of him."

Erin nodded. She may have been as uncomfortable as I was, but it was hard to tell. She and I wore masks. Bragg did not. Unconsciously, I stepped back.

"Dick, I thought you might like to have a word with your interpreter Diana—"

"Great, yeah. Tremendous to meet you. What do you think of all this? Tremendous, right? Bet you never thought you'd ever be part of something this absolutely tremendous in your whole life," he said despite the fact that I had been on the payroll for over six months and "met" him several times before.

Before I could say anything, he turned toward Erin.

"Time to put those nay-sayers in their place, eh, Erin."

Without waiting for her answer, he turned to me, grabbed my hand, and started to pump it. Erin gasped.

"Tremendous to have you onboard." He chuckled before adding, "Although, I've no idea why I pay so much for translation. After all, you've got the easiest job in the room. I pass you the ball, and we drive it home. You just be sure you say *exactly* what I say. You hear me?" he said eyes narrowing, still pumping my hand.

Well, happy Interpreter Appreciation Day to me. There was no point in telling him that an interpreter works with the spoken not the written word.

"I just need you to be…" he seemed at a loss.

"Tremendous?" I offered.

He smiled broadly. "Exactly."

Erin winked at me and managed to slip me an antiseptic wipe as she steered Bragg away. As I watched his retreating figure, disgust rolled over me. A stain had seeped into me that an antiseptic beach blanket would not cleanse. I tore open the foil package, extracted the wipe, and rubbed it aggressively over my hands. For a moment, I swore I smelled lavender, and my stomach lurched. I raised the wipe to my nose, breathing in somewhat more deeply because of the mask, but it was not the wipe. Its alcohol overwhelmed and erased any lingering scent, if one had ever existed at all.

Watching the path they cut through the room, gratitude welled inside of me for the woman responsible for wrangling the "man-child" behind One Test, the revolutionary blood testing system that could detect multiple bacterial and viral infections with one blood culture.

Though he would never admit it publicly, Bragg was a closet germaphobe. As far as I could tell, Erin followed him around all day with wipes. Reflexively, my hand patted the right-front pocket of my skirt. The gesture was met with a reassuring crinkle.

"Another one bite's the dust, eh?"

Startled, I turned to see Mary Nguyen standing beside me.

Her close-fitting black mask had stark white letters spelling out "One Test". A single drop of crimson blood hung in a permanent state of free fall just below the top-inner curve of the "O". Her heavily starched, white lab coat emitted a scratchy sound as she directed the "bye, bye" gesture to the soon-to-be-ex One Test employee.

"You heard from Hiro? The lab isn't the same without him."

I flinched and hoped she didn't notice.

"No. I haven't," I lied.

Her owl-like eyes blinked underneath the two round Os of her glasses, and for the first time, I noticed that the lenses were shaped exactly like the "O" in "One Test". Because of the mask, I couldn't really make out her expression, but I knew her well enough to be on my guard. She missed nothing.

"That's surprising."

"Not really. Not given the NDAs they have us sign."

She considered this with a sideways tilt of the head.

"I guess." She scrutinized me and added, "It is a bit Ye Olde Soviet Union here. Peoples' desks being cleared out in the dead of night, never to be heard from again. Still, I thought you guys were close."

"No, not really." I lied again. "After all, I'm just the interpreter." I glanced pointedly down at my watch and excused myself to do some prep work before the meeting started.

As I retreated, I couldn't shake the suspicion that her owl-like eyes tracked my every movement. I walked back to the videography and photo shoot area as purposefully as possible, marveling again at how Bragg had charmed his way into not only getting a meeting with the angel investor Ken Nishiyama, but also convincing him to let the presentation and demo be filmed. But, then, I remembered how he had sold me on the company at my interview.

"We're going to save lives. Imagine being able to do multiple lab tests with just a few drops of blood. It will be faster, easier, and cheaper. People won't have to rely on insurance companies anymore. We can make a tremendous difference in their lives."

And just like that, he sold it and I bought it—hook, line, and sinker.

Several feet behind the head table was a long advertising banner bearing the One Test logo on a field of black at the top and a smiling Bragg in his trademark red tie and black suit on a field of white at the bottom. Behind the banner was a utilitarian black chair on top of which lay a headset and receiver. A wave of petroleum-based ink assailed me as I took my seat. The banner must've been hot off the presses.

The young man, still unaware that by the end of the day, his keycard would be deactivated, his desk cleared, and his items packed, ready to be shipped home along with an ominous letter from the company lawyers reminding him in excruciating detail of the wide-ranging punishments for breaking the non-disclosure agreement, disparaging the company, or speaking with other employees, asked if I was ready for a sound check. He waved another headset in the air.

I placed my headset on, adjusted the mic, and gave him a thumbs up. He disappeared from view.

"Testing, testing, one, two, three," a voice crackled through the headphone. "Are you receiving?"

"Yes, I am," I said. "Can you hear me?"

"Yep, we're good to go. I'll just get Mr. Nishiyama set up."

Mr. Nishiyama spoke very little English despite investing in companies across the globe and always brought along his own interpreter, but Bragg had insisted that given the proprietary nature of the technology and the ever-present threat of industrial espionage that Mr. Nishiyama attend the first meeting solo and that One Test provide the interpretation.

"Thank you. Do you know if we are starting on time?"

"Should be. In about fifteen. Break a leg!"

Poor kid, he had no idea what was coming. With a pang, I remembered Hiro. His jet-black hair mixed with a high-bridged nose indicated his mixed-race heritage. His seemingly shy smile, a gift from his Japanese mother, belied the hearty laugh and wickedly wry sense of humor inherited from his

German dad. The last time I spoke with Hiro, he had not been laughing.

"Di, they frog marched me out of the lab," he said.

"What did they say?" It came out in a rush.

There was a long pause.

"They asked about Helen West."

I swallowed hard.

"I think they know." He had lowered his voice.

My skin prickled and a flush burned my face.

"But, how?" I searched my memory bank, silently running through the events of early spring. How, when my aunt felt unwell but refused to go to the hospital, I had convinced Hiro to include her blood sample in with other patients from the test launch at the large pharmacy chain under the pseudonym of Helen West. The relief that washed over me when the tests came back normal. I flushed again at the ridiculous pride I had felt at working for a company I could really believe in.

But it was all a lie.

Over the next few days, my aunt's condition worsened considerably. The pain in her abdomen intensified. Over-the-counter pain killers had no effect. Despite appeal after appeal, she refused to go to the hospital or be seen by a doctor. More than once, she grabbed my arm with a strength I would not have thought possible, stared at me unblinkingly, and demanded a promise not to take her to the hospital. She wanted to die at home. Time after time, I promised. Until, ultimately, I had to admit to myself that it was a lie.

I wasn't ready to let go. What if it were just a kidney stone? After all, the results of One Test had been normal. A call from her daily companion tipped the scales. An ambulance transported my aunt delirious with pain to the hospital, where they discovered that she had a perforated bowel. Her doctor's word rang in my ears: "If only you had come in sooner."

For the first week after surgery, no one could visit my aunt because of the COVID restrictions. I spoke with her on the phone in the morning and evening. She would alternate between begging and berating. But worst of all was when my strong, independent aunt sobbed like a lost child, paralyzed by the fear of permanent abandonment.

In the end, I brought her home despite her doctor and the hospital. For the next three days, I sat by her bed. Her insides were so rotten with infection that I had bought camphor-menthol ointment scented with lavender to smear on my upper lip. Its scent masked but did not eliminate the sickly odor expelled with each of her labored breaths. She slipped in and out of some form of consciousness as I administered liquid antibiotics for the infection and morphine under her tongue for the pain.

"Mommy, mommy, mommy," she would intone in that way that children, frightened by shadows at night, call out piteously for their mothers.

Early in the morning of day three, I gently rubbed her cheeks after dropping the morphine under her tongue, when she suddenly opened her eyes and stared reproachfully into mine.

"Why are you letting me suffer?"

Then, just as suddenly, she closed her eyes and slipped back into her nightmarish world. Her moans and ragged breathing my only guideposts. Her accusation, a punch to the gut. I'm not sure how long I sat there before deciding. The dawn imparted a rosy glow to the landscape beyond the bedroom window. I reached out, picked up the plastic bottle from the bedside table, drew out the clear liquid with the dropper, gently parted her lips, and squeezed out its contents under her tongue.

My aunt died an hour later.

Two hours later, I called her closest friend Sally.

"It was quite peaceful in the end," I said.

"Diana? Diana? Did you hear what I said?"

Hiro's voice was sharp.

"Bragg has to be stopped, but I can't do it. Someone has been following me, and I've been sent a cease and desist. I just can't afford to be involved anymore."

He sounded scared.

"You've done enough. Don't worry. You won't be hearing from me again," I said.

"I'm sorry," he said, but he sounded relieved.

"So, am I." I had just lost my only ally.

Despite my wandering thoughts, I could follow Bragg's spiel. I'd heard it often enough I could repeat it in my sleep. For all of Bragg's charm, he stuck very closely to a prepared script. Ad-libbing was not his forte, and he was paranoid about security. Of course, now I know why.

He'd just reached the point where he belittles researchers at an Australian university who claimed to be able to do a rapid COVID test with a mere 25 microliters, or half a teaspoon, of blood in 20 minutes.

"Half a teaspoon? Doesn't sound like a lot, but you can't get that from a finger prick," he said. "We've adapted our existing One Test to let us do the same testing for COVID with just a stick of a finger in minutes. Imagine being tested for COVID as easily as checking your blood sugar? Maybe the Aussies should stick to their barbies and leave medical research to the big boys, am I right?"

I softened the barb into a more palatable expression in Japanese. Part of the interpreter's job is to understand both the literal language and the intent. At times, intent takes precedence.

The best interpreters fade into the background, and people tend to forget that they are there, like a limo driver or a bartender. Sometimes they take a call. Sometimes they make a slip. Like the time a few of us had been preparing for a conference call with Mr. Nishiyama and Bragg received a call from a doctor about the accuracy, or more specifically, the inaccuracy of test results run on the One Test system.

"Listen, you moron, it isn't the test results that are wrong. It's your interpretation. Somebody reads the results, right? You make a diagnosis, right? And what is your diagnosis? It's just an educated guess, right? You know what defamation is, right?"

"Tremendous," he said as he slammed the phone down. His

beet-root face revealed a fury I had heard rumors about, but never encountered. Beneath the anger lay something else—fear.

His next call was to his lawyers ordering them to "fix it." The scary thing is they could. Bragg had deep pockets that doctors questioning the accuracy of One Test did not. The threat of years of costly legal actions appeared to be an effective deterrent. It was also enough for me to wonder about my aunt's test.

Bragg reached the demo part of his speech. Mary would prick his finger, collect a few drops of blood, and take them away to be analyzed. I breathed in deeply, removed my headset and emerged quickly from behind the banner when I stumbled into Bragg knocking the wipe that Erin had just passed him out of his hand. I apologized, retrieved the wipe from my pocket, and handed it to him. He ripped open the package and dabbed his bleeding finger with the wipe, and then held it there for a moment to make sure the bleeding had stopped.

Fifteen minutes later, Mary Nguyen re-entered the room in her crisp, white lab coat and reluctantly proffered the results to Bragg, who smiled confidently as he began to read the results. Her face betrayed anxiety. His smile faded. He gaped uncomprehendingly at Mary. She nodded gravely.

He was a man facing two terrible choices. He could save his vision or he could save himself. He hesitated before saying, "Well, I'll be damned. Sorry, folks. The test results say that I'm positive for COVID."

It was not COVID, but by the time Bragg had reached the hospital, the symptoms had progressed rapidly. On admission, he was suffering from a high fever, diarrhea, and disturbance of consciousness. In his delirium, he tried to tell the doctors, nurses, and anyone who might listen that One Test didn't really work and the results couldn't be trusted, but these protestations were met only with solicitous *there, there nows*. After all, one of the nation's largest pharmacy chains was promoting its convenience and reliability.

However, after the initial loss of time due to this overreliance on the supposed accuracy of Bragg's revolutionary testing system, his medical team started searching for an alternative cause for his rapid decline, but it was too late. He died several days later in isolation.

In truth, the likelihood of his survival was not high, but you can't say I didn't give him a fair chance. If he had come clean right away about the accuracy of the tests, he may have survived. All he had to do was to tell everyone that the test results couldn't possibly be correct. That they had been experiencing problems with the accuracy of the tests and the results were not reliable. To do that, however, would risk money that he desperately needed from his angel investor.

It is amazing the types of viruses, bacteria, and poisons stored in a lab like the one at One Test. You can even buy a machine to crimp a foil package from an online auction site. Of course, the newness of COVID and its wide-ranging symptoms worked in my favor as well.

Bragg's funeral was held a full three weeks after his death. At the request of his wife, no autopsy was performed. No one protested as neither the overwhelmed doctors nor the state had the time or energy to pursue cases of anomalies, so Richard J. Bragg was consigned to the ranks of one of the pandemic's many victims.

I met Erin for coffee the day before the service. We sat outside, enjoying the warmth of the mid-summer sun.

"She wants an open casket. Seriously, it's as if she wants proof positive that he is dead," she said, referring to Bragg's much younger wife Adriana.

The open-casket funeral scene from the Cary Grant-Audrey Hepburn movie *Charade* where two men check that Hepburn's con-artist husband is really dead using a mirror and a pin popped into my mind, and I tried not to smile.

Instead, I said, "It's funny how no one else tested positive for COVID."

Erin paused, her face leery, before steering away from the topic.

"I miss you," she said. "Things just aren't the same."

"We've been ordered to stop testing. Did you know?" She scrutinized my face.

I'd left the company pretty much right after Bragg's hospitalization, but rumors of a whistleblower had already started by then. The regulatory agency that oversees laboratory services had done a surprise inspection and requested a tour of the entire building, not just the company's cherry-picked labs. The inspection resulted in not only a regulatory audit but a financial one. The dominos of Bragg's long-con and sleights of hand had started to fall.

I'd put Hiro in touch with a college friend who is a lawyer representing whistleblowers. She would protect him.

"I did read a news article that questioned the accuracy of One Test results," I said.

Erin directed her gaze toward the skyline. She took a long sip of her coffee.

"Well, you know how it is, it's all a matter of interpretation."

Within the preceding weeks, the COVID crisis overshadowed news of the fraudulent manipulation of statistics by Bragg to hide One Test's dismal rate of accuracy. The pharmacy chain discreetly cancelled any outstanding orders, and the One Test company announced that it was changing its focus away from testing. It would now be taking on the challenge of developing pharmaceuticals for use in orphan diseases. That change in direction required new leadership. They wished previous management all the best in their new endeavors.

The next day, following the service, Bragg's wife officially thanked the hospital. Her eyes narrowed to slits as she said with a catch in her voice that she was sure that Dick would have approved of the new direction she intended to take the company. She brought out a dainty, handkerchief with scalloped lace borders and dabbed at her eyes.

After she had finished her remarks and greeted the more important people in the room, I moved toward her. Up close, her handkerchief appeared somewhat wrinkled but remarkably dry. She regarded me quizzically, trying to place me.

I reminded her that I was the interpreter at her husband's company. She nodded, thanked me for coming and peered less than covertly over my shoulder, perhaps, hoping for another more distinguished mourner to take my place.

"I'm very sorry for your loss," I said.

It was a lie, but it was one that I could live with.

After all, what are truth and lies but a matter of interpretation.

National Interpreter Appreciation Day is on the first Wednesday of May.

ONE STRIKE AWAY

BY RANDALL DEWITT

When a husband dies, most women clean out their closets. Clothes go to Goodwill or are unceremoniously dumped in the trash. Pictures get put into bins and stashed in the attic, or worse, framed and hung on walls in spare rooms no one ever sees. Lavona Godburn went a different route, leaving everything behind, and moving her and her eight-year-old son Derrick from rural Upstate New York to a Boston suburb. Time may be how memories become distant, but the way she figured, a couple hundred miles couldn't hurt either.

Finding work was easy. Lavona had served greasy food at a truck stop off the New York State Thruway for the better part of ten years and there were plenty of restaurants and diners looking for experienced waitresses in the Burlington area. Living on the meager salary and tips was another thing. As it was, Derrick felt like a leper in school. Being poor didn't help.

While none of his classmates were destined for "Hahvahd," none of them were a freak show oddity. Derrick had a birthmark shaped and colored like a wad of chewing tobacco dripping down his left temple, too long to be covered by his favorite baseball cap—a Yankees cap. With all the excitement of the Red Sox "Impossible Dream" season and the first two games of the '67 World Series against St. Louis about to be played at Fenway, wearing anything but a blue cap with a big red 'B' was blasphemy. Derrick might as well have been waving a Cardinals' pennant.

Still, Lavona thought it was absurd when his school sent a letter home *blaming Derrick* for not getting along with classmates. She'd hoped a new school would be good for him. So far, it wasn't.

Walking home from school the next day, Derrick took a shortcut through a sand pit, bypassing a steep hill and the herd of kids stretched along its upward slope of sidewalk. He was only yards from where the path entered the woods when he came across a few boys from his class. It was too late to turn back.

"What'd you say to me?" Derrick asked.

"Nothing," one of them answered.

"You were making fun of my birthmark, weren't you?"

The boy shook his head.

Derrick asked again but didn't wait for an answer. He hauled off and slugged the kid in the stomach, doubling him over. A second boy rushed in to help his friend but Derrick was too quick, sidestepping and tripping him to the ground. He booted the kid in the ass, then turned toward the last one in the group. That boy put his hands out to ward off an attack. It didn't matter. Derrick swung and knocked him down to join his friend. Satisfied, he left his three moaning classmates and continued on his way.

Once in the woods, Derrick took off his Yankees cap and picked up the first dried-out branch he could find. Using both hands, he gripped the straight piece of wood like a Louisville Slugger and took a couple choppy swings with it. Content with its strength and weight, he brought it up hard to his face, breaking it over his forehead above the right eye. He hoped for a welt but any mark would do when he told his mother the story about how *he'd* been jumped by kids from school.

When Lavona saw the knot over his brow, her heart sank. It

was New York all over again. And it was. Her son was a trouble-maker, never at a loss for a reason to beat someone up if he felt like it, just like the boys in the sandpit found out the hard way. Derrick had a mean streak, just like his father.

Before his death, Derrick's father often stumbled home nights with a split lip or mouse under his eye after stirring up trouble at the Albany area watering holes. Lavona could only imagine the things Derrick must've heard. His father's cursing and swearing at her in the kitchen, dishes or glasses shattering against the wall or floor, the slaps of his hand against her face. Possibly even the last time he'd threatened her.

"I don't want hotdogs and beans," his father barked, shoving away the dinner she'd put in front of him. "What am I? Six years old?"

Lavona grabbed the plate from their rickety kitchen table before it could be tossed toward the kitchen sink. He'd attempted that throw on numerous occasions, never once getting any tableware inside. It was the closest he ever came to helping with the dishes.

"Just once, I'd like to come home to a nice juicy steak."

"All we have is hamburger," she replied.

"Make me a burger then, rare, with American cheese."

"We don't have buns."

"Then put it on toast for Christ's sake," he snarled, adding, "and make it fast or I'll bury you behind the shed."

Lavona brought him a beer from the fridge. He snatched it from her, ripped the pull-tab off and flicked it at her. She looked at the near-empty ketchup bottle on the table and cringed. For a grown man refusing to eat a kid's meal, he'd been known to put up a fit if there wasn't enough ketchup to drown his burger in.

She pulled a paper towel off the holder and wiped the cast iron skillet, then crossed behind him and stepped on the trash barrel's pedal to open the lid and drop the balled-up paper inside. On her way back to the stove, she stopped directly behind him. She lifted the skillet and swung its rounded edge down hard to the back of his head.

Watching through the open crack of the kitchen door, Derrick winced.

Lavona put down the pan, grabbed a fistful of flannel shirt and pulled as hard as she could, toppling his chair over backward. His head bounced off of the cast iron radiator sending his limp body careening to the side. Blood pooled underneath his split skull by the back door of the house as Lavona washed the telltale evidence from the side of the skillet. Then, careful to watch where she stepped, she flitted around the kitchen wiping any blood droplets that splattered with a dishcloth. When she was done, she stuffed it into the pocket of her housecoat and headed Derrick's way. He slipped back into his bedroom without being seen. Then, he heard his mother's bedroom door close as the house went silent.

In the morning, Derrick woke to the sound of men asking questions in the kitchen. His mother was telling two state troopers she'd gone to bed before her husband got home and never heard a thing. She'd only discovered the body in the morning when it was her usual time to get up.

Apparently, they believed her. His death was ruled an accident.

~

DERRICK SWUNG his feet out from the covers and sat hunched over, hands rubbing his pounding hangover, before shuffling to the bathroom sink to splash water on his face. He squeezed what he could from a tube of Colgate onto his tongue and almost wretched, saved only by cupping his hand under the running faucet and taking a mouthful of water. After a quick swish, he spit out the foamy toothpaste and looked over at the chunks of Chinese food from the night before. He grabbed a wet towel from the edge of the bathtub and threw it over the pieces of chicken fingers and bits of beef fried rice between the toilet and the wall, and went back to bed.

Normally, his girlfriend Susan would've been the reason the

bathroom was a mess. She was a slob, with all her shampoos, conditioners, creams and whatnot scattered about on every free surface she could find. But she'd left days ago. She'd expected flowers on the anniversary of their first date and, not getting any, took it out on his bar tab that night drinking overpriced cocktails. He thought she'd gotten over it by the time they made it home, never mentioning flowers once in her ten minutes on top of him before passing out. He found out differently the next day when she sobered up. By day's end, she'd moved out, leaving the bathroom with just a bar of soap, a half roll of toilet paper and a wrung-out tube of toothpaste.

The problem was, Susan *wasn't* completely out of his life. The police wanted to talk to her to about a bar fight he'd been in a week earlier.

"That's my girlfriend," Derrick had warned the guy sitting at the corner of the bar, looking in the direction of Susan shooting pool.

"Yeah, so?"

"So, stop staring at her."

The sweaty shortstop had stopped into the bar to cool off after playing in a league playoff game. Dirt streaked the front of his softball shirt from a failed attempt to stretch a double into a triple in the fifth inning. He thought his outstretched hands touched the base before the tag was applied but the umpire called him out. He'd argued the call too far, muttered an obnoxious remark under his breath and had been tossed from the game. The only thing he was guilty of sitting at the bar was thinking his flop into third was safe.

"Go to hell," he told Derrick.

"What'd you say?"

"You heard me."

"Let's go outside and see you say that again, tough guy." Derrick motioned toward the door.

Still steaming, the ejected ball player wasn't about to back down, especially not to some shit stain in a Yankees hat. He didn't hesitate, leading the way out the back door. No sooner than they were outside though, a sucker punch dropped him to the ground. Derrick pounced on him, slamming his head off the pavement repeatedly in the dusking remains of daylight's final moments.

Derrick grabbed Susan and left. But unlike past bar fights, running off before the police could be called wasn't enough to avoid trouble. Someone in the bar recognized Derrick and the cops arrested him for the assault a day later. After making bail, there was no way he could afford flowers for Susan on her "special" night out, not as a roofer who couldn't hold a steady job.

Naturally, the police wanted a statement from Susan. Before their break-up, she would've backed his story. Now, there was more than a doubt. For all he knew, she wouldn't remember bending over the pool table to make a shot let alone lie and say the softball player had grabbed her ass. Without her help, Derrick's claim he was stopping her from being assaulted wouldn't survive the week.

Unfortunately for Derrick, neither did the guy he beat up. The local news identified the victim of the vicious bar attack as Jimmy Colebrook and went on to report he'd passed away without regaining consciousness. The police would be upgrading their charges to second-degree murder against the suspect in the fight, Derrick Godburn.

Realizing he was screwed Derrick went to a hole-in-the-wall bar and drank until they shut him off. After walking to a nearby Chinese restaurant, he was back in business, managing to get a scorpion bowl while waiting for an order. When it was ready, he sucked the drink down to the cubes, grabbed his takeout and took a cab home for the oriental food's destined encounter with the toilet and wall.

In a matter of months, the 27-year-old was sitting in a jail cell for killing Jimmy Colebrook, as the Sox were one strike away from winning the '86 World Series against the Mets. But then, a ball off the bat of Mookie Wilson dribbled through Bill Buckner's legs, costing the Red Sox the championship.

Derrick Godburn would've gladly traded places with Buckner.

~

Lavona was shopping at the Pheasant Lane Mall when Susan walked by, pushing a stroller. Despite how she'd testified against Derrick at his trial, Lavona was polite and said hello. Susan was nervous and said she could only talk for a minute. Still, it was ample time for Lavona to see the birthmark peeking out from beneath the beanie pulled down over the baby's forehead. Susan balked when asked the baby's name. It was obvious she didn't want Derrick to find out he was the father to a girl named Rose.

From prison, Derrick wrote Susan but never heard back. He wasn't surprised. She'd made it clear she never wanted anything to do with him again. In court, she didn't look his way more than once. Still, he continued to write in hopes she'd decide to let him meet his daughter. Years went by without a single visit from Susan and Rose McGill.

Being shut out of Rose's life was hard on Lavona too. She was in a prison of her own, paying for a crime she hadn't committed. Each Christmas, she sent Rose a card with a little cash in it. For all she knew, her only grandchild never even received them.

~

By the time Derrick served his sentence for second-degree murder and was paroled, he was no longer looking for trouble. Before prison, beating someone up was a way to make life interesting. Behind prison walls though, in places like bathrooms and recreation courtyards, fighting was a necessity. Clashes with other convicts over the years had landed Derrick in solitary, the prison infirmary or both. Now all he wanted was a quiet life and to finally meet his 23-year-old daughter.

First, however, he had to convince Susan his fighting days

were behind him. In prison, he'd attended counseling. He'd hoped it would convince her he'd changed. Enough, at least, so she wouldn't stand in his way of meeting Rose. In the end it didn't matter. Weeks after his release, he was standing in a doorway looking at his daughter.

Derrick had no problem picking Rose out of the crowd, thanks to her prominent birthmark, as people passed by with a hug, handshake or nod as they made their way toward Susan—or at least the humanly remains of her. Her body had been found ten days earlier in some bushes at Shedd Park.

~

SUSAN HAD MET Neil Tucker at an AA meeting and married him a year later. He told police he was at his band's practice the night she'd disappeared. By the time he got home, it was so late he claimed to have just crashed on the couch. In the morning, when he saw their bed was made, he assumed Susan had gone shopping or whatever else she usually did when she was pissed at him. With a smirk, he boasted it wouldn't be the first time she'd suspected him of sleeping around. According to Neil, women were always throwing themselves at him whenever his band played.

The lead detective wasn't amused, reminding him, "Well, this time your wife turned up dead."

Neil had a smug reply of his own.

"Yeah, and Derrick Godburn, the father of Susan's only child, just got out of prison and wanted to meet with Susan. You do the math."

After playing a voicemail from their home phone of Derrick wanting her to go out for coffee, Neil finished answering any other questions they had, then went to the funeral parlor to make Susan's final arrangements. Rose was glad she went along.

Neil had picked out a stained dress for the wake her mother hadn't worn in years. It was hardly a great choice. The torn underwear he'd chosen for her wasn't any better and the bra he brought had a broken underwire. It would've looked marvelous poking up through that hideous dress.

By the time Rose was through, she'd bought new clothes for her mother to wear and shamed Neil into having her cremated in the casket she was waked in. If he'd had his way, her mother would've gone into the furnace in a bunch of cardboard boxes patched together with duct tape. That way, there'd be plenty of money for the party he was throwing at the Hilton after the service for all the grieving funeral goers. According to Neil, Susan would've loved it. His band was even going to play for free.

To be honest, Rose didn't care what Neil did once the funeral was over. A respectful wake and funeral, that's all she wanted. But even that was too much to ask for. Days later, a half an hour into the wake, Neil's children from his first three marriages were making nuisances of themselves.

Neil's most recent ex-wife dumped her kids off, like it was an opportunity to go out without paying for a sitter. The younger of the two elementary school-aged children was smearing peanut butter on a bagel as his animated older brother played with a Game Boy.

His second wife, who was never any good at keeping tabs on Neil's only daughter, probably had no clue she'd gone to the wake on her own. The 16-year-old was sitting on a wooden folding chair, having trouble keeping her knees together in a much too short skirt. She'd also taken her shoes off to rub her swollen feet. Pregnancy will do that.

Finally, his 22-year-old son from his first wife was showing everyone his recent headshot and talking about moving to LA. According to him, he was going to be the next Travis Bickle, which wasn't all that improbable. In all likelihood, he'd end up a psycho taxi driver like the character DeNiro played and not an actor. He had about as much acting talent as his father did playing lead guitar and singing. Delusion was apparently hereditary.

For his part, Neil was bopping around in a new leather

duster, occasionally playing air guitar and doing leg kicks like he was performing on stage, and telling anyone who'd listen all about the wicked paint job he was going to have on his motorcycle's gas tank when Susan's life insurance rolled in.

"DIDN'T I tell you to not bother that poor girl?" Lavona asked.

Derrick turned around, surprised to see his mother standing there. She'd said she wasn't going to the wake. Then again, so did he.

"I knew you couldn't resist," she explained. "I was watching for you from the parking lot."

"I just want to give Rose my condolences."

"This isn't the way to meet your daughter... Besides, you look like hell. C'mon, I'll take you home and fix you something to eat," she said.

Derrick knew he was a disappointment to his 71-year-old mother. She'd always looked out for him and all he ever did was cause her aggravation and pain. Even now, he wanted to put up an argument. Reluctantly, he left without another word.

The ride to his mother's apartment building was silent. Neither talked. Both preoccupied with thoughts of the past and the prospects of what was to come. Then, as they pulled into her parking lot, Lavona smiled at Derrick and told him for the first time since he'd gotten out of prison, it was nice to have him home.

Lavona started a pot of coffee and stood between the kitchen and living room while it brewed. Derrick turned on the TV and was flipping through the channels to find the Sox-Yankees game. It was the first game of the last regular season matchup between the two teams. His Yankees were at the top of the AL East with about a five-game lead over the Sox in second.

"Rose is a beautiful girl, isn't she?" Lavona asked.

Derrick shook his head. "I feel bad about the birthmark. It's the only thing she's ever got from me."

Lavona waited for the coffee to finish brewing, then brought him a cup. He stared at the little swirls of steam that rose from it.

"What's wrong?"

Derrick didn't say anything.

"Something wrong with the coffee?"

"The police think I killed Susan."

Lavona wasn't surprised. "Why?"

"They have video of someone in a Yankees cap going through a Dunkin' Donuts drive-thru with her on the night she disappeared. They think it's me."

"Was it?"

"No, I called to ask her to go out for coffee that night, but all I did was leave a message."

"So, you have nothing to worry about," Lavona said.

"You don't get it. The cops say I had a motive to kill her because she testified against me."

"Well, her testimony did help put you in prison."

"But I didn't kill her."

"So, you have nothing to worry about," Lavona repeated.

"I have no alibi for the night Susan was killed," he replied, adding, "I only wanted to get together so I could to talk to her about Rose."

"Everything will be okay. Now come into the kitchen and let me fix you something to eat."

Derrick brought his coffee into the kitchen and sat down at the table where he could still see the baseball game.

"Is Shepherd's Pie, okay?" Lavona asked, pulling ground beef from thc fridgc.

Derrick nodded.

Lavona stepped behind him and brought a cast iron skillet down as hard as she could on the back of his head. If there was a video of him with Susan that night, he had to have killed her. At her age, she couldn't go through another trial. She'd tell the police he'd threatened to kill her too and only struck him with the pan to get away.

With a little luck, maybe, just maybe, Rose would take some pity and spend some time with her.

~

Thirty minutes had passed since Neil Tucker called the police to tell them Derrick Godburn was at the wake when a second call was phoned in, this time for a disturbance. The detectives on their way to the funeral parlor to make an arrest still hadn't arrived when officers from a patrol car entered the building. They were shocked by the chaos that confronted them.

Folding chairs were strewn everywhere. Two boys were crying, one with peanut butter all over his face, the other holding what looked like a smashed Nintendo. Nearby, a young man cursed and swore about ripped pictures, while a pregnant girl panted and complained about peeing herself. In front of the casket, a young woman with a birthmark had a man in a leather coat on the ground, punching him repeatedly. They pulled her off and cuffed her. As they led her away, she continued to call him a loser.

The crowd erupted in applause. Not because the police had arrested her, but because she'd kicked the good-for-nothing's ass and given his kids a well-deserved lesson in wake etiquette. They applauded even louder when the detectives cuffed Neil next, arresting him for the murder of Susan.

His story about how band practice went late into the night hadn't checked out. They looked at his cell phone records and found repeated calls to and from various women, one in particular—Amy Evans. When they brought her in for questioning, she admitted to an affair with Neil. After that, all they had to do was utter the words "accessory to murder" to get her to roll on him in return for a plea deal.

According to Amy's statement, Neil heard Derrick's voicemail and realized it was the perfect opportunity to get rid of Susan. Under the guise of working on their marriage, he had her stop for coffee that night before suggesting a walk together in Shedd Park. He strangled her when they reached a secluded stretch and dumped her body in the bushes. Neil only told Amy afterward. He wanted her to be the next Mrs. Tucker, although she already had the feeling he was cheating on her.

Susan always used her debit card at Dunkin's and Neil knew it'd lead the police to a video of her car in the drive-thru with a passenger with his head down, wearing a Yankees baseball cap. Between the voicemail, the video and a picture Neil dug up of Derrick wearing a Yankees cap, they'd have to come to the conclusion Derrick was the passenger. But it didn't work out that way. Amy told the police right where they could find the baseball cap when they executed a search warrant at her house, right where all their lives ended up—in the trash.

~

Rose McGill moved as soon as it was possible. She didn't go far. Only far enough away that she wouldn't have to drive past Shedd Park very often or the funeral parlor where her mother was waked. Far enough she could go out without being "that poor girl" from the murders.

That fall, the Sox lost to the Angels in the American League Division Series and the Yankees went on to win it all. Rose didn't care who won. She'd never been a fan of baseball.

Rose did, however, buy a baseball cap. She wears it on weekends to remind herself of the father she never met and the grandmother she never plans to visit in prison. She puts her hair into a ponytail and pulls the hat on, not caring how much of her birthmark it covers.

~

May 15th is Vascular Birthmark Day.

MURDER IN THE WINDS

BY CAROL KAUFMAN

Kiki Coben walked through the rooms of her new house, dodging furniture in need of arranging and piles of cartons awaiting unpacking. Luckily, Kiki was an organizational wizard, and every box was labeled clearly as to its contents. She had started on the kitchen first thing in the morning. After all, they had to eat. She would unpack the bedroom next. After all, they had to sleep.

But first, she needed a cup of coffee. The aroma of freshly brewed Ethiopian Genika filled the kitchen and beckoned her to the espresso machine on the counter.

Kiki had taken the week off from her job as the food columnist at the *Sherwood Gazette* to deal with the move, so setting up her office over the garage could wait. But not for long. One of three sisters who had shared a bedroom, she, like Virginia Woolf, had always dreamt of having a room of her own, and now she'd have one. In her head she sketched the design for the cozy, light-filled office—so inspiring for writing the Great American Novel. That is, when she wasn't answering readers' questions about bread flour versus all-purpose, or the difference between yams and sweet potatoes.

The doorbell rang, rousing Kiki from her reverie. She navigated around the carton maze to get to the front door, where she found a towering woman with wavy auburn hair holding a plate of brownies.

"Welcome to Calla Circle! I'm Phyllis Bacon. My husband Jeff and I live across the street, in the yellow house," she said, turning and pointing with her plate.

"Thank you so much! I'm Kiki Coben. Please come in. I just brewed a pot of coffee. Would you like some?"

"No, no. You're too busy. I'll just stay a few minutes."

Kiki took the plate of brownies and set it on a table, then pushed some boxes aside with her foot to give access to a chair. Phyllis sat down.

"So, how do you like it here? Or is it too soon to tell?" Phyllis asked.

"I've always loved this area of town," Kiki said. "It's so leafy green and peaceful."

"You grew up here in Sherwood?"

"Yes, in the Cottage Farm neighborhood. My sisters all left town, but I came back after Tim and I got married. My parents still live in the same house I grew up in."

"This really is a great neighborhood, and the cul-de-sac makes for a very friendly atmosphere. We do a lot together," Phyllis said.

"Like what?"

"Barbecues, pool parties, yard sales. The guys play poker. You don't happen to play mahjong, do you?"

"No, I don't, but I've always wanted to learn."

"I'd be happy to teach you. We have a group that meets on Tuesdays. We've had a space at the table for a while now and we'd love to fill it."

Kiki considered the invitation. "I guess it would be good way to meet the neighbors," she said, but wondered about privacy in the small cul-de-sac.

"And make some new friends. We're meeting at Dale Valenti's house on Tuesday afternoon at two. She's in the blue house. Can you come?"

"Sounds good. Are you sure you can't stay for coffee? I'd

love the company, and I can't possibly eat all these brownies by myself."

"You've convinced me," Phyllis said and followed Kiki, brownie plate in hand, into the kitchen.

~

PHYLLIS WAS WAITING on Dale's doorstep when Kiki arrived at exactly two o'clock the following Tuesday, holding a tray of baklava. Phyllis led her into the family room, where two other women greeted her with big smiles.

"Hi. I'm Dale Valenti," said the shorter of the two, a blond with bouncy curls and the deepest dimples Kiki had ever seen.

"Jane Darcy," said a woman with salt-and-pepper hair cut in a blunt style. "Phyllis tells us you're a beginner."

"Totally!"

"Don't worry, we'll teach you. We've been desperate for a new player," Dale said, her chocolate brown eyes glinting as she eyed the pastry. "You may be a beginning mahjong player, but you're obviously an advanced baker."

"I have to be advanced. I write about food for the *Gazette*," Kiki said.

"You're that Kiki?" Dale exclaimed. "And is that baklava you're holding?"

"I hope it's okay I brought it. I've been testing recipes all week and have a ton of pastry in the house."

"This could be a fattening game," Dale said. She took the plate from Kiki and set it down on the credenza. She and Jane each snatched a piece.

Dale moaned. "This is so delicious. The honey and the nuts..."

Jane tsked. "And the butter!"

"Is your husband also a writer?" Phyllis asked.

"No, Tim's a firefighter."

"Ooh. That's exciting," Dale said.

"And dangerous, Dale," said Jane, shaking her head.

"Of course, it is," Dale said, chastened. "Your house must have all the super-duper detectors."

"It will. Tim's over there right now supervising the electrician."

"I guess you'll be safe," Jane said.

"That's the plan."

The four women took their places around the table and Phyllis began to explain the rules of the game. "Unlike Chinese mahjong, the American game has cards that show the permitted hands. I'll share mine with you until you can get your own."

"The cards and the hands on them change every year," Jane added, "so it's not like gin rummy, where you can make up your own from the cards you're dealt."

Phyllis continued. "We use these racks to hold our tiles. The suits are called craks, bams, dots, winds, and dragons. There are also jokers."

Kiki laughed. "Crak and bam! It sounds like an old Batman comic book fight!"

Phyllis laughed and said, "Why don't we just start to play? I'm sure you'll pick it up more easily than if we keep reciting chapter and verse."

"Good idea," Jane said. "Let's get moving. First, we stack tiles into walls in front of our racks."

With the sound of tiles clicking softly on the game table's green felt surface, the women went to work setting up the game.

~

The following Tuesday, Kiki came through Phyllis's door holding a leather case. She set it down on the coffee table.

"Look what I found in a closet," she said, clicking open the latches. "It's a very fancy mahjong set."

Dale sat up in her chair. "This is Macy's set," she said, gazing sadly at the case. "Macy Stannard, the woman who lived in your house."

"I haven't met either of the Stannards," Kiki said. "Only the attorneys were at the closing."

"You know the reason they sold the house?" Jane asked.

"Um, no," Kiki said.

Jane took a dainty sip from her teacup. "She left Matt."

Kiki's eyebrows went up. "What happened?"

"Too good-looking and charming for his own good. Or for his marriage," Jane said, her mouth pursed. "Matt's a hound dog, plain and simple."

"Ouch," Kiki said.

Phyllis agreed. "Macy was always suspicious about his extra-curricular activities, and she confronted him at least once about them."

"What does Matt do," Kiki asked, "besides playing around?"

"He's an insurance salesman," Phyllis said.

"That's where his charm is so valuable," Jane said. "And you mean he *was* an insurance agent."

Phyllis explained. "Right. After Macy left in the middle of the night, he spiraled downward and lost his job. He went on a real bender, drinking and gambling, and plowed through what savings they had."

"Until he saw the writing on the wall," Dale added. "He sold the house before the bank could take it."

Jane pursed her lips again. "He really let the place go to hell. Even if he couldn't manage to fix the broken shutter that's been hanging there for ages, you'd think he could at least have mown the lawn and trimmed the hedges once in a while."

Dale agreed. "Especially since Macy was so particular about the landscaping."

"The lawn was okay when we looked at the house," Kiki said.

"That's because Jeff mowed it when the agent told us she was bringing you by. Macy was particular. She's a florist, you know. She had Floribunda downtown."

"Until she sold her half to her partner," Jane said.

"Matt was really upset when he told us about that," Phyllis said.

"I hate to admit it, but I was glad he sold the house. It was really bringing home values down," Phyllis said.

"I was ready to burn it down if he hadn't," Jane snapped.

Dale flashed a look at Jane. "That's not nice, Jane. Can't you tell he's suffering?" Her voice strained and her eyes teary, she said, "We should play with Macy's set today. I didn't realize how much I missed her until I saw it."

"And we can raise a glass to her and her new life," Phyllis said, lifting her coffee cup.

Dale picked up the case and spilled its contents onto the card table.

"What *was* strange was that the agent said he chose to sell to us even though our offer was below asking price," Kiki said.

"Why would he do that? To give less of the proceeds to Macy?" Jane asked.

"Apparently because we said the place was perfect. Frankly, we were so happy to get the house—and at that price—we didn't question it," Kiki said. "Now we can afford to paint the place and do the renovations right away."

Jane huffed.

"You have to admit, Jane, that it must have been horrible for him to wake up one day and find his wife gone. He must have been distraught," Dale said.

Phyllis nodded. "He was pale and shaking when he came over here to tell us. We had to give him a big slug of Scotch to calm him down—at breakfast."

Kiki finished placing tiles onto her wall. "Where did Macy go?"

"We don't actually know," Phyllis said. "But she always said that if she left, she was never coming back. And we figured she'd get in touch once she got settled."

"Gone with the winds, huh?" Kiki said.

Dale started to laugh but choked, shooting coffee out of her nose. Phyllis jumped up to pat her on the back.

Jane ignored them. "Macy knew that Matt could charm somebody into spilling the beans. Somebody who would feel sorry for him." She glared at Dale.

"But we do feel sorry for him, don't we Phyllis?" Dale said. "Kiki, Matt's staying here with Phyllis and Jeff."

"That's so kind of you," Kiki said. "But I haven't noticed him in the neighborhood."

Phyllis waved her hand in dismissal. "It's only for a short while until he can get himself settled in a new job and find a place to live."

"Do you think Macy might've gone off with somebody?" Kiki asked.

Dale's eyes flashed. "You mean like a boyfriend?"

"I don't think so. We would have known if there was somebody," Phyllis said.

Jane shook her head. "Macy was never one to keep a secret. We knew every last detail about her marital woes."

"And Jeff is their lawyer. He would've heard something," Phyllis said.

"But she kept leaving town a secret, didn't she?" Kiki said.

The three women looked at each other and shrugged.

What kind of person would just leave without telling her closest friends?

"How long has she been gone?" Kiki asked.

"Gee," Dale said, gazing off into the distance. "It's gotta be six months now. We did think about looking for her but didn't have a clue where to start."

Jane interrupted. "Dammit. We're missing a tile."

"We'll use my set." Phyllis rose from her chair and went to a cherry wall unit to retrieve her game case.

Jane looked up at Kiki, a frown creasing her forehead. "I'm curious. Were there any problems in passing papers?" she asked.

"Not at all. The sale went through without a hitch."

Jane persisted. "I wonder how they got the deed notarized if Macy wasn't around."

"Jane, just because Macy hasn't been in touch with us doesn't mean she hasn't talked with Matt," Phyllis said.

Jane grumbled.

"I actually saw the notary's stamp," Kiki said.

"What a funny thing to notice! What made you look at that?" Phyllis asked.

"Nostalgia, probably. My dad was a notary. I used to take the stamp out of his desk drawer and stamp my homework papers. I loved running my fingers over the bumps."

"How sweet!" Dale gushed.

The sound of the front door opening startled the women into a quick silence. A man breezed into the family room with a big grin.

"Hello, mahjong ladies!"

"You look happy today, Matt," said Phyllis.

"Good news makes me happy. As of Monday, I have a new job at AllStar Insurance, and to top it off, I've found a great condo downtown that I'm sure Macy's gonna love."

"That really is good news, Matt," Dale said. "Congratulations!"

"Thanks. So, what gossip do you have for me this week?"

"Well, this is our new neighbor, Kiki Coben," Phyllis said, tipping her head toward Kiki. "She and Tim are what's new in the neighborhood."

"Right. Good to meet you. How are you enjoying our house?" Matt asked.

"We love it," Kiki said. "Good to meet you, too."

"Perfect, I heard you called it," Matt said.

"They're planning some fabulous renovations," Dale said.

Matt's eyes widened. "Oh yeah?"

"Dale, why don't you let Kiki tell him?" Jane said with an eye-roll.

Kiki smiled. "We're turning the space over the garage into an office for me."

"Don't forget Tim's project!" Dale reminded her.

Kiki laughed. "Right, Tim is getting himself a man cave in the basement."

"Wow. I've always wanted one of those," Matt said. "I guess our house wasn't so perfect after all."

Dale interrupted. "Kiki found Macy's mahjong set in the house."

Matt's eyes filled with tears, making his ice-blue eyes gleam.

"Oh, my God. Macy loves that set. She never would've left it behind if she meant to stay away. This is fantastic news! She's planning to come back to me. Today's turning out better every minute!"

Kiki saw Phyllis frown. Dale's cuticles demanded sudden attention. Jane blanched.

"Listen, I know what you're thinking. I screwed up royally, but I've learned my lesson. I love Macy and I want her back in my life. If she left that set behind, it means she'll be back."

On that note, Matt turned on his heel and practically floated out of the room.

Jane leaned over the table and whispered, "Is he delusional? Macy. Is not. Going back. To him."

Kiki looked down and pretended to rearrange her tiles, wondering how Jane could be so sure. *What does she know that Matt doesn't? Has Jeff told her something?*

~

KIKI WENT OVER and over the conversation at the mahjong game in her mind. Her reporter's instinct told her something was off, and that something weighed on her mind. Why would Macy Stannard have left a family heirloom behind if she was really leaving her husband? In fact, did she plan to come back?

The question deserved an answer and Kiki decided to do some investigating.

Just because I write about food doesn't mean I've forgotten everything I learned in journalism school. A little adrenalin surge would be nice. It's been too long.

~

A TALL, lanky man with a warm smile opened Floribunda's door at precisely ten o'clock on Wednesday, and Kiki was suddenly struck with a case of nerves. What was she doing playing detective? To calm herself, she browsed the store, picking up a primrose here, a jade there, reminding herself that she was a trained journalist. Her courage restored, she chose three African violets in shades of pink and purple.

As she handed over her credit card to the man, she introduced herself and asked, "Are you the owner?" she asked.

"Yes, I'm Paul Claremont." His emerald eyes sparkled.

This guy is gorgeous. Maybe Macy went off with him?

"My husband and I just bought Macy Stannard's house. I understand you were partners."

Claremont looked at her over his reading glasses and frowned. "That's right. What can I do for you?"

"Do you know about Macy's mahjong set?"

A look of surprise shot across Claremont's face. "Great-Granny Emma's? Sure I do. Why?"

"She left it in the house. I'd like to return it to her and thought you might have an address."

Paul Claremont's eyes dimmed. "I don't have an address."

Kiki persisted. "Have you heard from her?"

"No. Macy will call when's she's ready. She does things on her own schedule. I used to call her Spacey Macy when she'd forget to do something." He paused before saying, "Although I have to say I'm a little pissed that she hasn't even sent me an email. She knows I would never tell Matt where she is. I don't fall for his so-called charm."

He placed Kiki's purchases into a cardboard box.

"Why did she leave?"

Claremont scooted around the counter and began to move planters around in the front window.

He's fidgeting. Those plants don't need rearranging.

"Macy said she wanted to start the next stage of her life."

Kiki gathered up her plants, thanked the florist, and was

about to leave the store when she had another thought and turned around.

"Did she ever tell you she was afraid of Matt?"

"No. She was just fed up with his screwing around. I never did see what she saw in him."

"So, you think she just left him?"

"That'd be my guess." He picked up a potted geranium and began to pluck dead leaves from it before heading back to the counter.

"I've never met Macy, but I'm curious that she left without telling anybody, and that she left behind the set."

Claremont leaned forward and placed his elbows on the counter. "She used to say that one day she would leave his cheating ass behind. But Great-Granny Emma's set? No. That's not like Macy."

"What is like her?"

"She'd want to make Matt crawl."

So maybe she really is planning to come back.

Kiki thanked him and left the shop. More curious than ever, she headed straight to her office, where she sat down in front of her computer and tapped in the URL for the state corporate database. Once on the website, she typed in the name of the flower shop. After about ten seconds, Floribunda appeared on the screen. The owners were listed as Macy Stannard and Paul Claremont.

No wonder he was so fidgety. Macy didn't sell her half of the business. What is the man hiding?

~

THAT EVENING, as Kiki chopped carrots, her eyes were focused on the cutting board, but her mind was elsewhere.

Tim broke into her musing. "You're awfully quiet tonight, babe. Something on your mind?"

"Why would Macy Stannard leave that mahjong set in the closet? It doesn't make sense."

"Uh, you want to fill me in?"

Kiki described the morning's conversation with Paul Claremont and her discovery that Macy hadn't actually sold her share of the business to him.

"Maybe Macy just wanted to teach Matt a lesson and she really is planning to come back," Tim said.

"That's what Paul Claremont said. But how much can one woman take?"

"From what my cop buddies tell me, they take a lot."

She needed some information, and she knew just where to get it: Tim's poker buddies, a bunch of firefighters and cops.

"Where are you playing cards tonight?" she asked.

"Denny Fisk's. Why?"

"Tell them all to come over here instead. I'll make all their favorite snacks."

"That'll certainly get 'em here. But why?"

"I need to ask Keith Berman a question."

"You're not going to play Nancy Drew again, are you?"

Kiki bristled. "I am a reporter, you know."

"I know you are. But prying into other people's business could get dangerous. Remember what happened last time? We had to call animal control to help get you out of that tree."

Kiki laughed. "That *was* one nasty dog chasing me. But you have to admit I got the job done. I found the missing thumb drive."

Tim groaned.

"Anyway, I just have a question about police procedure." Sensing Tim's hesitation, she said, "Don't worry. I'll make the guac you love."

"Okay. I'll text the guys."

~

WHILE THE MEN played cards in the den, Kiki bided her time in the kitchen researching recipes. Her editor wanted an article on how many ways a home gardener, aka said editor, could make use of a ridiculously abundant zucchini harvest. She knew it was just a matter of time before beer and salty snacks did their job, and she was right. About an hour into the game, she heard a chair scrape against the floor and caught a glimpse of Keith Berman as he headed toward the bathroom. Poised on the edge of her maple Windsor chair, she waited until she heard the faucet in the sink turn off, then jumped up to meet him in the hallway.

"Keith, can I ask you a question?"

"Sure. What's up?"

"Are police complaints public record?"

"Court records are published if something goes to trial, but not complaints, unless there's a really big crime. What're you looking for?"

"Do you keep a record of missing persons reports? I'd like to know if somebody filed a report about his wife disappearing."

Keith frowned. "Is this woman a relative or friend of yours?"

"No. I've never even met her, but she used to live in this house. None of her friends has heard from her."

"Had she ever threatened to leave before?"

"Well, yes. Her husband fooled around, and she told friends that one day she'd leave."

"Well, there you have it. She left."

"But there's more."

Keith's eyebrows went up.

"Her great-grandmother's mahjong set."

"Huh?"

Kiki told him about the mahjong set. "Why would she do that? If she had planned to leave, wouldn't she have packed everything she wanted ahead of time?"

Keith nodded. "Anything else besides a hunch?"

"Is there any record of domestic violence?"

"Give me the names. I'll check it out. That's a really bad business," he said.

Bad business for sure.

An idea struck Kiki. "Do you think I could get a hold of the agreement she and her partner signed when they went into business together?" she asked.

"Why?"

"If there's a survivor's clause, then Paul Claremont wouldn't have to buy her out. He'd just have to wait for her body to show up."

"Well, there's a leap."

"I think I remember Phyllis saying that Jeff did their legal work."

"Kiki, if you really believe that Paul Claremont is involved in Macy's disappearance, you'd better leave it to the police. This could get very dangerous."

"Don't worry. I'm not going to confront him alone."

"And their lawyer will never share confidential information."

Kiki shrugged. *How can I convince Jeff to let me see that agreement?*

THE NEXT DAY, while Kiki was pulling a zucchini bread out of the oven, the phone rang.

"Kiki? It's Keith Berman."

"What did you find?"

"Nothing. No complaints filed, from either party. And no missing persons report."

"Hmm. Thanks, Keith. I really appreciate your help."

"You sound disappointed."

"Maybe I am."

Kiki hung up and processed what Keith had told her. She was surprised to find herself frustrated. Was Tim right that she just wanted to play girl detective? Maybe Macy Stannard had simply gotten tired of putting up with her husband's tomcatting and left.

But what about that mahjong set? She had to hand it to the woman. If she was planning to come back, Matt was certainly learning his lesson.

~

"ARE you all unpacked and settled in?" Jane asked the following Tuesday. She trailed Kiki into the kitchen, surreptitiously running a finger across the dining room sideboard to check for dust.

"We're getting there. We had an architect over the other day to talk about changes."

Jane snorted. "You probably should have done this before moving in."

"I know, but our lease was up, and we didn't want to carry both the mortgage and the rent for another year."

Dale and Phyllis appeared in the doorway together. "Is that chocolate I smell?" Dale asked, her dimples deepening. "What did you bake for us today?"

Kiki laughed.

"I had salad for lunch. Feed me now," Dale pleaded.

Kiki went into the pantry and returned bearing a tray. "This week we have chocolate rugelach, in honor of International Mahjong Day!"

Happy moans filled the room.

"August first may be my favorite holiday ever!" Dale said as she reached for a piece.

"By the way, look what I found," Kiki said. With a flourish she pulled a mahjong tile from her pocket. "It's the missing one."

"Where did you find it?" Jane asked.

"It was stuck between some loose floorboards in the bedroom."

"Was that where you found the set?" Dale asked.

"Yes."

"Shall we play with Macy's set then?" Phyllis asked.

"We'll have to. The one I ordered won't arrive for another three weeks," Kiki said.

"Why buy one? Until we hear from Macy, let's just use hers," Jane said. "It's not as if you're going to give it to Matt."

The women took their seats around the card table.

"Speaking of Matt, he suggested the other day that we schedule a bowling night," Phyllis said.

"We should! We haven't played in a while," Dale said.

"Since Macy left," Jane said.

"Kiki, it's so much fun. The guys are really competitive, and we just laugh a lot," said Dale.

"Tim and I actually love bowling. We met at an alley in college."

"Great," Phyllis said. "I'll ask Jeff to set it up."

Dale held a tile for a moment before discarding it. "You know, Macy's great-grandfather brought this set back from China in the 1920s. It's made of bone and bamboo. Just look at the carvings and the images."

"The workmanship is absolutely beautiful," Kiki said, running her fingers over a tile intricately engraved with a flower symbol.

"I think I finally have a hand!" Phyllis called. She plucked a four-dot from the middle of the table and set it on top of her rack with three identical tiles.

"The set's probably worth a lot today," Jane said.

Kiki's head snapped up. "Really?"

"Sure. It's not just a hand-me-down. It's an antique," Jane snapped.

"All the more reason she wouldn't have left it behind," Kiki said.

The clacking of the tiles stopped and the women around the table stared at Kiki.

"You don't believe she's planning to come back?" Dale asked.

"I don't know Macy at all, but you're her friends. Don't you think it's a little odd that she just disappeared without telling you? And that she left behind one of her most precious possessions?"

Phyllis turned to Kiki. "What are you saying?"

"I'm really not sure."

"Kiki, give the set to me," Jane said. "First thing tomorrow, I'm calling an antiques appraiser. I want to know just what Macy left behind. She may have been telling a tall tale about the set. It might just be a good plastic knock-off."

~

SATURDAY NIGHT, Kiki needed an excuse to stay behind as the others headed out to the bowling alley, so she blamed her editor for a last-minute change to an article. Once she saw the cars leave Calla Circle, she went to the junk drawer in her kitchen and pulled out the key to the Bacons' house. She scooted across the street and let herself in.

On the theory that legal work for neighbors might be in his home office, she went straight to Jeff's desk to search for the key to his file cabinet. It was sitting in plain sight, next to a pile of paper clips in the organizer.

Smart, Jeff.

She slid the key into the lock and finding the file she wanted, pulled it out and laid it on the desk.

Oh, Jeez. Just what I feared. There is a survivor's clause in this contract.

Kiki put the file folder away, locked the drawer, and put the key back in its place before heading out to join the group at the bowling alley.

~

MATT ARRIVED halfway through the first game, out of breath and with wet hair.

"Sorry I'm late. I had a squash game I completely forgot about, and I really needed a shower," Matt said.

"That's okay. By the time you check in and get your shoes on, we'll be ready for a new game," Chuck said.

"I've really missed these bowling parties," Matt said as he pulled off his street shoes. "Getting together with you guys reminds me of happier times." He stopped to choke back some tears. "When Macy gets back—"

Dale cut him off mid-sentence. "She'll be back."

Poor guy. Matt is a lot more sensitive than I would have expected from a chronic philanderer. Maybe it's Macy who has something to hide.

Kiki saw Jane's eyes roll as she mouthed the words, "Could his cologne be any stronger?"

"Can we set up some regular get-togethers?" he asked.

Chuck clapped Matt on the back. "Sure thing, buddy."

Tim picked up a ball and positioned himself on the lane. Just as he brought his arm back in preparation for releasing it down the alley, his cell phone rang. He groaned and lowered the ball onto the rack before pulling the phone out of his pocket. He looked at the Caller ID and frowned.

"It's the station. What could they want?" A moment later he turned to Kiki, his face contorted. "Our house is on fire!"

Kiki and Tim grabbed their belongings.

"Give us your shoes. We'll return them and follow you back," Jeff called.

Within minutes they were back at Calla Circle. Even before his pickup truck had come to a full stop at the head of the street, Tim opened the door and jumped out. Kiki ran after him. Within seconds she began to choke on the heavy black smoke pouring from the house and raised her arm over her face.

The street was filled with fire engines, police cars, and an ambulance. Firefighters in full gear worked in a smooth team operation to connect hoses and extinguish the blaze.

Captain Joe Ross spied the couple and loped across the lawn and onto the pavement. He extended his hand to shake Tim's, then clapped him on the shoulder while directing the couple backward, away from the inferno.

"Where did the fire start?" Tim asked.

"We'll know more once we get in there, but we definitely smell gasoline."

"Gasoline? Does this mean it was set?" Kiki cried. "But we have the monitored alarm system!"

"I'm so sorry, but whoever set this fire did it with a mind to make it spread quickly. It looks like a total loss."

Kiki's knees buckled. Tim caught her as she fell and eased her onto the Bacons' front lawn. They grasped each other's hands and stared at the flames devouring their new house. Tears rolled down Kiki's face.

~

WITH A LOUD AND ECHOING CRASH, two trucks set down large green dumpsters in the driveway early the next morning. Minutes later, a hazmat-suit-clad crew showed up. Their goal was to sift through the ruins to find clues as to the cause of the arson. And perhaps to the arsonist him- or herself.

Her computer having gone up in flames, Kiki borrowed a legal pad and pencils from Phyllis and parked herself in a deep red Adirondack chair on the Bacons' front lawn. Tim chose a forest green one next to her. She plugged her earphones into her ears and selected the most calming music she could find on her phone's playlist to counteract the clamor of charred wood being tossed into the dumpsters. But writing did not come easily. The stink of burned house assaulted her nostrils.

About an hour in, Kiki sensed movement out of the corner of her eye. She looked up to see one of the workers staggering out of the rubble. Tim jumped up and rushed across the street to meet him.

"What's happened?" Kiki asked, coming up to the two men.

"You'd better stay here," Tim said.

"No, I want to see. What's going on?"

Tim followed the worker toward the pile of embers that had been their house, Kiki right behind. Workers congregated in the middle of the ruins, frantically pulling blackened beams and wallboard from a small area within the house and flinging them in all directions. As she reached the backyard, Kiki spun toward a retching noise emanating from behind a tree. A man was vomiting into a rhododendron bush. Suppressing a gag reflex, she jerked her head away and turned back toward the house. She gasped.

Lying in the rubble of the basement were the charred remains of a human body.

THE DOORBELL RANG the following day. Tim found Joe Ross and another man standing at the front door.

"This is Bernie Glover," Joe said by way of introduction.

"Of course. The state fire marshal," Tim said, extending his hand. "Do you have an update on the investigation?" He led the way into his in-laws' living room.

Kiki was seated on the floor, looking through old family photo albums. She stood up when the men entered.

"We didn't touch anything," she said by way of greeting.

"That's what I would've expected. But you didn't have to stay with your parents. Insurance would've paid for a hotel room."

"This is much better than a hotel," Kiki said. "Besides, Mom and Dad are on a cruise right now, so we have the place to ourselves."

"I guess that would be better."

"So, what's your take here?" Tim asked.

"This was definitely a case of arson. There was a lot of accelerant," Glover said. "Do you have any idea as to who might want to do this?"

"Not a clue," Tim said.

"Is there anybody you've had a problem with lately?"

"Not that I can think of."

"No problems at work?"

"No. Everybody at the station house is terrific."

"What about you, Kiki? Any enemies?"

"God no," Kiki said. "I write about food."

"What about the neighbors? Any disagreements over fences or noise?"

"No. They're our friends. They were at the bowling alley with us," Tim said.

"I'll need the names and contact info for everybody you were with that night, and anybody you think might have had been angry enough to set fire to your home."

"I'll make a list." Kiki stood and headed toward a drop-leaf desk. A few minutes later, she handed a sheet of paper to Glover. "Here are the names and telephone numbers of the people we were with," she said, "and everybody we work with."

Glover glanced at the list of names and scribbled something in his notebook.

"Who, besides you, has a key to the house?" Glover asked.

Kiki sighed. "I was supposed to call the locksmith to change the locks, but I got so busy with work that I kept pushing the appointment back."

"Again, who has a key?"

"The Bacons, the Darcys, and the Valentis. That we know of. But they were all with us at the bowling alley," Kiki said.

"And Matt Stannard," Tim added. "He and his wife Macy were the previous homeowners."

"Mrs. Stannard doesn't bowl?" Glover asked.

"Macy left town. Matt was staying with the Bacons until just a few days ago," Tim said.

"But are you sure the person used a key? Couldn't somebody have broken in?" Kiki asked.

"I suppose that's true," Glover acknowledged while scribbling in his notebook. He looked up. "Are you sure Mrs. Stannard isn't around?"

Kiki and Tim exchanged puzzled glances. "What do you mean?" Tim asked.

"If Matt Stannard has a key to the house, wouldn't his wife also have one?" Glover asked.

"What are you getting at?" Kiki asked.

"The body found in the house was a woman's," Glover said.

Kiki reached for Tim and grabbed his hand. "Do you know who it is?" she asked.

"Not yet. The medical examiner is running tests, but we think it's Macy Stannard."

"Why?" Tim asked. "What would've been her motive to burn our house down? She had a problem with her husband, not with us."

Glover kept writing.

"Wouldn't she have seen how different everything looked?" Tim asked. "That different people lived there?"

"Not in our basement, Tim," Kiki said. "There's nothing there except the washer and dryer and a pile of paint cans. It looks exactly the same as when we first looked at the house."

"Gasoline was poured upstairs, too." Glover said.

Kiki scrambled to find a reason, but chaos raged in her mind. "It was well after sunset when the fire started. Maybe she never turned the lights on."

"Unless she didn't know he'd sold the house," Glover said. "You did say she'd left him."

The notary seal.

"But Macy Stannard's name was on the deed. How could she not have known the house was sold?"

Where was Paul Claremont tonight?

"Um, I did sort of interview Paul Claremont," Kiki said.

"Who's he?"

"He was, or is, Macy Stannard's partner in the flower shop."

"What does that mean?"

"I heard that Macy sold her half of the business to him. But—"

"But?"

"When I checked the state's corporate website, she was still listed as co-owner. Maybe you should check on their relationship."

But don't look too closely into what I've been up to.

"But why would he burn your house down? What's the motive?"

"I don't know, but he acted kind of squirrely when I talked

to him. Maybe you should look into Macy's partnership agreement with him."

Tim's eyes opened wide.

Uh oh. I'm gonna hear about this after Ross and Glover leave.

As soon as Glover left, Kiki headed to the den to use her mother's computer, reminding herself to go by the mall to pick up new laptops for herself and Tim. She pulled up the Registry of Deeds website and scrolled through until she hit pay dirt.

"Bingo," she said, pumping her fist. She pulled her cellphone, a notebook, and pen from her hobo bag and printed out a copy of the deed. Then she wrote down the notary public's name. Logging out of the registry's site, she searched for a listing of notaries in the area. She found what she was looking for, made another note and, stuffing everything back into her bag, logged out of the computer and ran to her car.

Twenty minutes later she knocked on the door of a brown-shingled Craftsman house on a quiet street in Burston, a bedroom community about 25 minutes from Sherwood. A petite redhead answered the door.

"Are you Dana Norman, the notary public?" Kiki asked.

"Yes, I am. How can I help you?"

"Actually, you notarized the deed to my house. I have a couple of questions about it." She pulled the paper from her bag. "Do you remember notarizing this?" she asked.

The notary took the paper and squinted at it. "That's my stamp, but it's not my signature."

"Do you recognize the names on the document?"

The notary squinted again and blushed. "Oh, my God."

"What's the matter?"

Silence.

"I believe I'm entitled to see your journal," Kiki said.

"Of course." Dana stood and went into the house, returning

a few minutes later with her record book. Her hands trembling, she opened it and checked it for entries on that date.

There was nothing.

Phyllis did say that he burned through all their savings. How desperate he must have been to have forged Macy's signature.

"How do you think this happened, Ms. Norman?"

Her face crumpled. "Somebody must have taken the stamp when I wasn't looking."

"Somebody? Like Matt Stannard?"

"Matt and I are in love. We're getting married after his divorce."

"And that excuses his forging her signature—and yours? You may end up not only paying a huge fine, you may lose your certification," Kiki said, almost feeling sorry for the woman.

Dana folded into herself as she sank onto the front step.

"I wouldn't go out to buy a wedding gown just yet," Kiki said.

~

KIKI WENT THROUGH HER PARENTS' house, busying herself with putting sheets on the beds and straightening up the living room. Normally Tim's 24-hour shifts at the fire station didn't bother her, but since the fire she didn't like being alone.

The mahjong group was coming to stay with her. Although her first instinct had been to say "no, thank you" to their offer of company, Tim convinced her to change her mind.

"It'll be fun for you all. A good ole pajama party."

"I'm actually looking forward to it now. We'll play mahjong."

"They're probably expecting a gourmet meal."

"Gourmet? They're getting pasta."

Her tasks completed, Kiki headed to the kitchen to start the marinara sauce. The aroma of chopped onions and garlic sautéing in oil soon filled the kitchen. After pouring the tomatoes, tomato sauce, wine, and some herbs into the mix, she paused, an open bottle of cayenne pepper in her hand. Remembering that Jane didn't like spicy food, she decided to leave it out and set the bottle down on the counter.

The medical examiner had confirmed that the body in the basement was Macy Stannard's. Kiki understood that Macy must have been furious that Matt had forged her name on the deed. But she couldn't understand why she'd punish her and Tim by burning down the house.

She heard the front door open and breathed a sigh of relief. Her friends had arrived.

"Come on in! I'm in the kitchen," she called. She listened for female voices laughing and chatting, but there was nothing. She went through the door into the foyer and found Matt Stannard blocking her passage.

"You should keep your doors locked, Kiki."

"Matt, I wasn't expecting you," Kiki said. She turned and headed back into the kitchen. She tried to keep her voice calm, but her gut was telling her she needed to be wary. This so-called charming guy had forged his wife's signature and sold their house without her knowledge. "Tim'll be here soon. Do you want me to call him for you?"

"He won't be coming home tonight. I saw him at the station when I drove by."

Kiki swallowed.

"I heard a rumor that mahjong set's worth something. I want it back."

Of course. It's always about the money.

"I don't have it, Matt. It must have burned up in the fire." *Did Jane get the set back from the appraiser? I can't let on.*

Matt slapped Kiki across the face, sending her reeling backwards into the refrigerator. The stainless steel door felt cold on her back. Her cheek stung.

The truth suddenly became clear to Kiki. She knew she had to keep him talking. She also needed a Plan B.

"So that whole story you told about Macy leaving you was

just that, a story, huh? The more you talked about her coming back, the more we'd all believe that you really missed her."

"It sure kept people from asking questions."

"How did it happen, Matt? How did you kill her? Did you plan it? Were you really going to marry the notary?"

"It was an accident, I swear. And no way was I going to marry Dana."

"How'd it happen?"

"I came home and found Macy packing her things. She said she was fed up with my screwing around. I lost my cool and grabbed the mahjong set she was holding. We got into a tug-of-war. I pushed too hard. She fell backward and hit her head on the corner of the dresser. That damned mahjong case broke open and stuff scattered all over the floor."

So that's how the tile got separated.

"So why didn't you call an ambulance?"

"She was already dead. I panicked."

"So you wrapped her body in plastic and buried her in the basement?"

"Yeah."

"You deluded yourself if you thought that nobody would ever do anything to the house," Kiki said.

"You said the house was perfect," Matt hissed. "You can't trust anybody anymore."

"What did you do with all her stuff?"

"Since everything was already packed, I just brought it to a Goodwill center," Matt said. "Far away from Sherwood."

"But you kept the mahjong set. That charade took planning."

"Yeah. And now I want it back. It's worth good money."

"And I'm telling you I don't have it. You're welcome to search the house." *And while you're doing that I'm going to run like hell.*

"Do you think I'm stupid?" Matt slapped Kiki so hard her head bounced against the refrigerator door. Her ears rang. He began to pace the room.

"But you're smart, Matt. Even if killing Macy was an accident, you recovered fast enough to plan a cover-up."

"I'm good at recovery."

"Except that now I know what a liar you are. And a forger. And a killer."

"But you're not going to be around to tell anybody, will you?"

Kiki shivered. *I have to keep him talking while I figure out how to get away.*

"You know, if you hadn't lost your job, you never would have had to sell the house," she said.

"Yeah, and nobody would ever have found her."

"At least until you died and new owners decided to renovate. So, when you heard about our plans, you had to move fast."

"You bet. I didn't want anybody digging up old Macy."

"And that's why you wanted the bowling party. It was the perfect opportunity to break into our house."

"You've figured this all out, huh?"

"You bet I did. That so-called squash game was another lie. You needed a shower to wash off the gasoline smell."

"I told you. I'm smart. I'm good at calculating."

The doorbell rang.

"Hello, Kiki! We're here!" Dale's voice. "What smells so good?"

Then Jane, who muttered, "Kiki, you really should keep your door locked."

At the sound of the women's voices, Matt turned his head toward the front hall and Kiki took her chance. She lunged toward the counter and, in one swift and smooth motion, lifted the bottle of cayenne pepper from the counter and flung its contents at Matt's face. Blinded, he cursed and flailed his arms, trying to find his way to the sink to rinse his eyes. Jane rushed into the kitchen and, judging the situation, raised the mahjong set high and brought it down onto Matt Stannard's head. He collapsed onto the bamboo floor.

THE DOORBELL RANG JUST as Kiki and Tim were sitting down to dinner. Kiki got up and went to the foyer. On the front step stood the mahjong group. Behind them was Paul Claremont.

"We wanted to check in on you and see how you're doing."

"I'm better now that Matt Stannard is under arrest. The DA said he'll probably go to prison for the rest of his life."

Tim came up behind Kiki and put his arms around her. "We owe you all an enormous thank-you for helping Kiki."

"She did all the heavy lifting," Phyllis said.

"But Jane delivered the knock-out punch," Kiki said.

"That old set really is worth its weight in gold," Dale said, eliciting a laugh from the friends.

"We never would've learned what happened to Macy if not for the fire," Phyllis said.

Kiki sighed. "Every time I close my eyes, I see Macy's charred body. I don't think that image will ever go away."

"As calculating as Matt thought he was, he didn't do his homework," Tim said. "He was wrong if he thought Macy's body would be burned to ashes in the fire. A cremation oven works at a minimum of 1400 degrees. A house fire only reaches about 1100 degrees."

"And to think Macy Stannard herself was almost blamed for the fire."

Paul interrupted "And what about me? You sicced the police on me."

Groan. "I'm really sorry about that. But when I saw that Macy's name was still listed as your partner, I jumped to conclusions." *To say nothing of that survivor's clause. And I mean that. Say nothing!*

"Yeah. I've been a bit overwhelmed since I've been on my own. I just haven't gotten around to changing it. I showed the cops the big check I wrote to Macy months ago."

"The least I can do is write an article about your shop," Kiki offered. "Maybe we can find you a new partner."

"Deal."

Tim and Kiki exchanged glances.

"Kiki and I'll be moving," Tim said. "That place has too many bad memories for us now. Let somebody else build on the lot."

The friends were silent, alone in their thoughts.

Phyllis looked up, hopeful. "But will you still play mahjong with us?"

Kiki smiled and threw her arms around the other three women. "You bet your bams!"

August 1st is International Mahjong Day.

COMMENCING MURDER

BY DONNA RICCI

Peter Morley sat in the dark in his musty office of the dampest stone building on the Valley Star University campus. The wood in the room smelled like an old church, last August's waxing now a memory as the heavy wood bookcases and beams had no luster in early June. Peter's large collection of books also stank, as did the spare tweed jacket he kept on an antique coatrack some of his students once gave him. The odor drove him nuts. He smelled it everywhere. Reflexively, Peter whiffed the poplin shirt he was wearing to see if it held the musty aroma as well.

"Lavender, damn it." He swilled cheap vodka in a heavily-fingerprinted Waterford highball glass, engraved with his name and year, another gift from students.

It was quiet in the building. Most of the grad students who had inhabited its halls were either done with their tomes, or working at one of the local restaurants. The undergrads were done for the year and had fled days earlier. Every sound was magnified, and he thought he knew them all: the squeaking front doors, the clunking elevator that caused the lights to blink as it opened its doors on every floor, the distinctive footsteps of certain people, and even the way the wind pressed hard against old windows, letting in random bursts of air. These were his sounds and he waited for them, acknowledged them, and was comforted by them. He guzzled another mouthful, and before he could feel guilty, poured another.

Peter dozed off. The heavy glass fell to the oriental carpet, but did not break. The thud woke him, causing him to groan.

"Damn it." He picked up the glass and placed it on the side table. He was sitting on his worn leather sofa, hadn't moved from the same spot since before sundown. He stood and sat down again.

"Damn it." He coughed and spit into the glass, missing it a little. He hung his head and breathed into his hands for several minutes. Then he reached for the vodka bottle and finished its contents.

He took off his loafers and sprawled on the sofa, using two embroidered pillows under his head, a souvenir from students who went to Turkey and the mohair afghan won in last Christmas's Yankee Gift Swap, even though he hated the lint it made. The crummy air conditioning vent was over the sofa and the blast of cool air landed on him. He fell asleep in a semi-fetal position and did not wake until daylight.

The early summer light made him groan as he checked the mantle clock on his bookcase. He got up anyway. The professor had a bathroom with a small shower attached to his office, so he took advantage of the hot water and shaved as well. He made a cup of coffee from his sideboard. He washed the Waterford glass and cleaned the table where his spit had landed.

It was silent and to his thinking, he was the only one in the building. He kept hearing soft footsteps anyway and went to the office door sticking his head out expecting to see someone but didn't. He smelled lavender again, and sniffed his clean shirt reflexively. It only smelled like starch and hot iron.

"Damn it."

His students, Henry Bostick and Ruby Quinn, were on his mind. They were tied inextricably to him, and probably forever. The one could ruin his career; the other could ruin him. The office telephone rang, startling him.

"Professor Morley," he answered.

"Good morning, Professor Morley, it is Mrs. Professor Morley wondering where her noted husband spent the night and with what tasty morsel."

"Oh, hi, Caroline. I got a little drunk and fell asleep in my office. I was too blitzed to think about calling. Everything okay?"

"Yes, now that I know you aren't dead. Did your TA remind you that graduation is tomorrow and tonight is the baccalaureate? Is he there already? He makes a point of telling me how he always beats you in."

The professor groaned.

"Are you coming home to change, or do you want me to bring clean clothes and your robes?"

"I'll come home, probably in a little while. I have an appointment with a student, indubitably to receive yet another gift of gratitude. Then that's it. We'll go to the service tonight, the faculty party after, and the graduation tomorrow. After that, you and I will set our own land speed record to Cape Cod and we'll remain on the Cape until August. At least. I'm so exhausted."

"Oh goody. Two months in a cottage with a drunk, sulky old professor. I will be sure to pack the vodka and lawn chairs. If nothing else we can see how early you get drunk every day and then keep a graph of the summer booze you consume to bring to the October AA meeting I am making you go to. Bye."

"Goodbye." He put the ancient receiver back in its cradle slowly. She was a piece of work. She was a piece of something else when she took his breath away at a church supper wearing a tight black pencil skirt and a sheer white blouse with a lace slip underneath and those funky red high heels. She was just 19 and he was almost 30. To boot, her father was very wealthy and generous to her and to him, too. He had a lot to lose if she ever learned about Ruby.

The coffee wasn't helping, so he made another cup. Sitting at his desk, playing absently with his pen and sipping the thick joe, he thought he felt the air of a person moving but when he turned, he was alone. He wanted more booze, but knew it wouldn't help. Now, if his appointment was on time, he could get out of here once and for all. Maybe for all. It would depend on how his summer turned out.

He felt the movement of air again, thought the window behind his desk might be open, and he turned to check. The quad outside was the last thing he ever saw as the marble mantle clock cracked the side of his head wide open.

~

IT WAS an unnerving spring for Professor Peter Morley. He was drinking too much and forgetting things. Jack Frye, his teaching assistant and master's candidate, kept him on an even keel professionally. Morley's personal life was a little more precarious.

In the professor's office, Jack worked on the papers from Morley's in-basket, skimming Henry Bostick Jr.'s copious doctoral dissertation draft over and over. Full of weighty prepositional phrases and obscure diction, it was a difficult paper to read and not at all like Bostick's conversational jargon. But in the end, paragraph after paragraph made no sense because there were no theories, no opinions, and at least three prepositional phrases in each sentence.

"What a load of crap," said Jack aloud. He threw the heavy paper on his desk. As he did, a colored sheet fell out. It was a handwritten note from the professor.

> *Henry, this paper is specious, it proffers nothing, it offers no proof of, well, anything. We need to talk. Please make an appointment to see me immediately. It is crucial that we speak.*
>
> — *PROF. MORLEY*

Jack sat back in his chair, blew out a huge breath. He placed the document and note in a worn brown interoffice envelope. He then dialed Henry's cell and went directly to messages.

"Hi, Henry, this is Jack from Professor Morley's office. He has some comments on your dissertation. I'll leave it in the Department mail box for you to pick up today. Take care. Call the office if you have any questions or need to make an appointment with Morley."

~

PROFESSOR MORLEY DRUMMED his fingers on the old desk, leaving fingerprints on the damp wood. He was trying to think but he could not pull himself together enough to center his wild thoughts. *Focus, old man.* He opened his file drawer and pulled out a flask, a garish Art Deco silver one presented to him by the Fitzgerald club a few years back. It was his office spare and today was full of his usual vodka. He took a hard swig and put it away, then filled his mouth with breath mints. Vodka doesn't smell, but it does. A knock on the door made him swallow the Tic Tacs *en masse.*

"Damn it," he said softly, then he bellowed, "Enter!" Henry Bostick, Jr. came in. Eight was much too early to discuss anyone's dissertation let alone his.

"Morning, Professor. How are you? Glad another summer is almost here?"

"Sit down, Henry. I have some disturbing news for you."

"Sir?"

"The doctoral review committee has made some allegations about the research in your dissertation. Apparently, your sources are confined to one arena, namely the Perpetua study at the University of Central Illinois, and they had commented on that in an early draft and insisted you widen the scope of your background research, which you failed to do, despite the fact that Valley Star has comprehensive research tools at your disposal. They also intimated the possibility that you plagiarized the analysis of Perpetua's research and that you did not conduct your own studies. As proof, they refer to your bibliography which is scant at best."

"Professor, this is insane. Why would they suggest such a thing?" Henry's face reddened and his eyes twitched. "Why are they saying this?"

"Easy, Henry. The committee insists that you provide the material you have gathered in your own research, regardless of its condition—notes, scribbles on napkins, anything to solidly prove you have conducted the research you said you did and do so in the next 24 hours. The committee also alleges that the conclusions you drew about the period, the literature, the society are the ones presented in the doctoral dissertation on the Central Illinois website. You must—"

"Don't I get the benefit of the doubt? I've been here since my freshman year. I've achieved honors and been published."

"You have the benefit of our doubt because we are affording you the opportunity to show us the basis of your work, to show us that your work is indeed new and well-thought out."

"But—"

"Henry, a doctorate from this school will be worth nothing if we send out a paper with questionable origins or a speck, a whiff of doubt as to its quality and importance to the field. With the issues brought up by the committee, we would be leaving ourselves wide open. I have been here longer than you and have no intention of in any way tarnishing the school's reputation. So my advice to you is to cooperate, come clean if you have to, regroup and then perhaps rework your studies. You don't have a lot of choice."

"Sir, this is outrageous. I've gone into debt for tuition, spent years completing these studies, and to have my work questioned on the whim of a committee, three quarters of whom know nothing about literature…" He was shouting and his face was red, a different red than the professor's. "I stand by my work. I will fight this."

"Henry, you cannot fight this. Your responsibility as a doctoral candidate is to defend your work. You *have* to defend your work. Do what the committee requests, provide the information they need. Rework your dissertation based on their comments and instructions."

"Will you go to bat for me with them, tell them my work is solid? You believe that, don't you?"

"In the face of what they've suggested, I'm inclined to stay out of this. You haven't shown me much, you haven't confided in me. I won't be able to give you the endorsement you think you deserve. Please go home, give the committee what they want, and then spend a day or two thinking through how you'll proceed. I've been given the task of informing you that you will not receive your PhD at the commencement this spring. There is nothing more to say. If you think of any constructive questions, call or come by, but please be sure to first respond to the committee's requests."

"I was counting on a teaching job in your department in the fall."

"The job opening posted on the doctoral student website was for any interested doctoral candidates to apply. You didn't. Three others did and one got the job. The student finished and defended a superb study of literacy in the Industrial Revolution. Your expectation is amiss. Sorry, my boy."

"I hold you responsible for this," Henry shouted. "You let me dangle in the wind, you did nothing to help me. I won't forget this. You won't forget this." Henry stood as he spoke, all the while glaring at the professor. Then he stormed out.

Jack was coming up the hall with coffee for himself and his boss. He heard Henry's diatribe, his threat to the professor, and grinned. Henry pushed by Jack as if he had not seen him. As he entered the office, Jack saw the professor drink from the vodka flask.

"Morning, Professor."

"Morning, Jack. So what's up for the day?"

"Uh, you have a teleconference with Rob Silver's parents. They are calling regarding this letter we sent." Jack gave a copy of the letter to the professor.

"Hmm. Do I want to fail him?"

"No, you want to give him an incomplete and grade him when the fall semester starts provided he submits papers for the two assignments he cheated on."

"How magnanimous of me. Why?"

"He had mono for the entire second term. His father is an alum and has given five grand a year for the last ten years."

"Ah. What else?"

"I got your comments on Henry Bostick, Jr. to him. I told him to contact us if he wants to talk to you."

"He came in earlier. Not a happy camper right now."

"And the lovely Ruby Quinn wants you to send her the Word file of her thesis today so she can get it printed and bound."

"I suppose."

"The underclass grades are due this morning."

"That's your department."

"They're done, sir. I need you to sign off. You can do it online but I also did a paper version, here. Sign this." The professor dutifully signed the paper without looking at it.

"How'd your students fare?"

"Ok, a few As, lots of Bs, and one D."

"Softhearted bastard."

"No, good teacher. Besides, failing English Comp 1 would not bode well at their stage of life." Jack smiled. The phone rang, and he answered on the first ring.

"Professor Morley's Office, TA Jack speaking. How can I help you?"

"Christ, this ain't Harvard, Jack," moaned Morley.

"Yes, good morning, Dean Wainwright, he's right here."

Morley grabbed the phone.

"Morning, Walter, what can I do for you? Yes, she is. Yes, a master's candidate. I understand she's getting it ready for the printer. She's bringing it around today for its final look-see. Can I give her a message?" Morley grimaced. "No, Walter, the work is done, it's verified. Jack here has read it cover to cover at least ten times so not even a comma is out of place.

"Yes. I already wrote a letter of recommendation to the school district where she wants to work. Glad you checked. See you at the Baccalaureate." He slammed down the phone. "Jack, once that woman is out of town, I'm getting plastered."

"What now?"

"The dean got an email saying her work was not original."

"Well, sir, technically it isn't."

"Yes, but only three of us know that, and since one of the three researched and wrote most of the damn thing for her, I am curious who sent the email."

"You think she's blabbing to her friends?"

"Are you nuts? She has a very lucrative, well-paying job waiting for her. Why would she throw that away? I didn't send the email. That leaves you. Did you send it?"

Jack's face twisted. "No sir, I wouldn't do that."

"Well, you have a thesis in progress, perhaps you want a free one too."

"That's ridiculous. You want a fresh coffee?" Jack slammed the coffee pot and mugs as he brewed.

"No thanks, I have a meeting I'm going to be late for if I don't get going." The professor rushed out of the office although his meeting wasn't for hours. He didn't have the time or emotional energy for Jack right now.

~

RUBY QUINN and Peter Morley sat across from each other in the Hog Penny Pub, a block from campus. Dark and woody like an English country public house, it was filled with students, professors, locals, and a few parents and teens in for campus visits. Sixties folk music played from Alexa, not too loudly, and a sign on the tiny stage advertised the live entertainment to come that evening, a Weavers tribute group. Peter drank Scotch on the rocks, doubles. He was on his third glass. Ruby drank mineral water and lime as she picked at a salad. They didn't speak, just stared at each other, sometimes it looked like glares, and sometimes it looked vacant. When Ruby finished her lunch, they were going to the Holiday Inn in Brockton. Not the best place, but far enough away.

"You going to finish that salad? You've been stirring the lettuce around for a while now."

"I guess I'm not too hungry. Did you finish the paper? I want read it. I may have suggestions, you know. My own words. I need, well, you need to finish up so I can concentrate on the baby. I feel good now but, who knows? And I have to get ready to move to Chicago and take birthing classes and talk to my lawyers. It's a very busy time for me."

"Your lawyers? I thought we were squared away. I have no more money to give you, Rubes. Christ, you'll be making more than me in a couple of years."

"I need the baby to be protected. I need his father's name on the birth certificate. You understand that don't you?"

"You have to understand the difficulties that could make for me down the line if it were known. I told you I would think about this but honestly, I don't see what good that will do. I've agreed to give a one-time cash payment and fund a little annuity until the baby is an adult. Eighteen, I think."

"Twenty-six, so he can go to college."

"Really?"

"That's one of the things we need to change. My insurance guy put me wise to that. He can be on your health insurance until then too. Or mine, if it winds up being better."

"Insurance guy? Yesterday you talked about your real estate guy. It's a no for my health insurance. What other guys do you have?"

"What do you mean by that?"

"Nothing…"

"If you think that I—"

"Forget it. You and I have been together almost four years. It's wild that you didn't get pregnant till now."

"Let's not do that again. I've been on the pill forever and

sometimes girls get fibroids and things and the whole thing gets screwed up. It happens, you know."

"And of course, a bright young career woman fresh out of a master's program decides to keep the baby, have it all, in fact. A kid, a plum job, and a pregnancy while her erstwhile English professor writes her thesis using absurd, hardly defendable research conducted before you got knocked up. This should be a master's marketing psychology case study. Maybe I'll write it. I'll change the names to protect the guilty."

"Bastard. I'm going back to school. I'm in no mood."

Peter threw money on the check, finished his drink, sucking up the ice cubes and spitting them out when he got to the sidewalk.

~

On the day of Professor Morley's murder, Jack Frye was uncharacteristically late. As he approached Professor Morley's office, he balanced a steaming paper coffee cup, a heavy back-pack, and a pile of bound reports in his left arm as he fiddled loudly with the key he used every morning. The back-pack, laptop and papers, crashed to the floor.

"Dammit," Jack cried loudly to the empty hallway. He unlocked the door at last, swinging it open and announcing, "Good morning, Professor." He put down his coffee, pocketed his key, and dumped the reports on his desk. He slammed the door, looked around at the sunny office, which looked so much brighter in the mornings. His desk, less grand than the professor's was neat as a pin. Morley's desk looked like a cyclone hit it.

He walked back to the office door and opened it. Then he made his way to the space behind Peter Morley's desk to open the windows and air vents. "Oh dear God," Jack cried. "Oh dear God."

He picked up the phone on Peter's desk and punched 899, the campus police's emergency number.

"Campus police, this call is being recorded. Dial 2 to reach the desk officer." Jack dialed 2.

"Officer Sullivan here, what is your emergency?"

"Teddy, this is Jack in Morley's office. He's on the floor behind his desk and the side of his head is bloody. I think he might be dead."

"Jesus. I'll call 911."

Jack sat for a minute at Morley's desk. He opened the file drawer normally kept locked and took out a couple of bound documents, carefully sliding them into his back-pack. He also took out a leather pouch. Petty cash. There was about $4,000 in it as students repaid emergency loans before heading home for the summer. Jack took the cash, stashing it in his own wallet. "That'll about cover all the coffees, Peter." He heard movement in the elevator so he sat on the visitor's chair next to the desk.

"Jack, Jack?"

"In here."

Teddy paled. "Christ. Whatta ya supposed happened?"

"Beats me, maybe he hit his head on the desk."

The commotion of three EMTs coming out of the elevator was next.

Teddy went to the door to flag them. "Over here."

The EMTs whistled in unison.

One of the EMTs held the professor's limp wrist and shook his head. "This man is deceased." He looked toward Teddy. "You'd better call the local police. This isn't a university police-type matter."

Twenty minutes later, Detectives Tom Engle and Dave Hathaway flashed their badges. Three uniforms stood behind them.

Blood from Professor Morley's wound coagulated to a deep wine color, almost black.

"Who found him?" Detective Engle was looking down at the body, not addressing his question to anyone particular.

"Jack did," said Teddy.

"Jack?"

"Jack Frye. His teaching assistant."

Detective Engle followed Teddy's extended arm to Jack and addressed him. "You normally come in this time of day?"

He nodded. "Yeah, I do but today I got in just a few minutes ago. The professor's an early bird and I try to be in before him, bring us good coffees before we start on the crappy coffee machine. Get the day set up right, you know. Today, I had to bring my car in…" Jack paled and started to sweat. "I've never seen that much blood before."

"Teddy, get him some water. Take it easy, son. We'll get him taken care of. You better wait outside." Detective Engle put his hand on Jack's shoulder.

"No, I can't leave the office, leave his papers here."

"Is that your desk?" Detective Engle pointed to the desk with the backpack."

"Yes."

"Sit there then and don't move, don't touch anything, got it?"

"Yes." Jack sank into his chair.

"So, Jack. Anything in the office missing?" Detective Hathaway asked.

Jack looked around. "Not that I can see. This is just an office full of papers and junk and fleas." Both detectives walked around the room, observing. Detective Hathaway came to the dreary bookshelves, looking at dusty old leather-bound books intermingled with dusty new contemporary paperbacks and a pile of new hardcovers. On the middle shelf there was a bare space with no dust.

"Jack, what's missing here?"

"Damn. That was where his marble clock was. Big, grey ugly thing."

"Get pictures before the medics touch him, search the office, closets, files and cabinets. What's behind here?" Detective Hathaway opened the door to the little bathroom where Professor Morley had showered just a couple of hours ago. "Jesus! A freaking shower in his office? Have them take a look in here too."

They heard a commotion at the elevator.

"Let me in. What's going on?" The uniforms tried to prevent Dean Wainright from entering the office. He halted at the door and saw his security officer and the teaching assistant. "What the hell happened here, Frye?"

"I found him when I came in."

"When was this?" Dean Wainright was looking at the body the entire time he spoke to Jack.

"Around nine. I was late today.

"Has anyone contacted Caroline?"

"No, there's been no time. Should I?"

"I'll take care of that. It might be easier for her coming from a friend."

Engle told Dean Wainright not to notify her. They'd deliver the news.

"What have we got here!" Detective Engle pointed to dark red drops of blood on the faded hall runners in the hallway. The uniforms came and put down an evidence marker, took pictures, and collected blood samples. Detective Engle followed the blood to an opening in the wall that looked like a dumbwaiter. When he pulled its door handle up it moved with ease. The inside was dark, dusty, and full of dead beetles and spiders, and in the middle of it, there sat on its side a gray marble mantle clock.

"Well, boys, we've found the professor's clock." The uniforms quickly surrounded the dumbwaiter, photographing the clock from every angle, dusting every surface of anything and everything, and finally tagging and bagging it to take away.

Detective Engle went back into the office. "Did the professor have any visitors yesterday or today? Anyone scheduled to come in?"

"Well, let's look at the calendar," said Jack as he pulled a black leather book off the professor's desk. "Hmm. Yesterday, a doctoral candidate came in. Henry, Henry Bostick. Oh and the professor had lunch yesterday, I think with Ruby, a master's candidate he's been seeing since she was a freshman. Good friends."

"Benefits?" Detective Engle lifted his brow.

"I never asked."

"Why would the professor shower here? Playing squash at the faculty gym?"

"There's no faculty gym," said Jack sarcastically. "Sometimes, the professor drank too much and fell asleep where he landed, most often in the office. The shower was here from when it was the Dean's office before the remodel. He just found it handy."

"What department is this?"

"English."

"Can I get a list of his students?"

"Sure. I'll print one out for you. Wait. Here's the graduation list. This is some of them." He handed the detective proofs of the program for the college's commencement.

Engle scanned the list. "I don't see that Bostick kid's name. I thought you said he was graduating."

"He is a doctoral candidate. From what I gather, his dissertation wasn't accepted. That's why he met with the professor. To get the bad news. He wasn't pleased."

"How do you know?" Detective Engle watched Jack twitch before answering the question.

"I was coming back with my breakfast as their meeting ended. I heard him shouting."

"What did he say?"

"All I heard clearly was that it 'wasn't over'. I was coming down the hall and thinking of an egg and English muffin sandwich."

Detective Hathaway was looking over the disheveled piles of mail on the professor's desk. "What a mess. A lot of personal mail here. Why would he have his bills and statements sent here?"

"Don't know."

"Look at this. A mutual fund account in his name only.

Whew. My wife would never let me get away with that! And a bill from the Ob/Gyn Department at Beth Israel in Boston. Is the missus having a baby?"

"No kids."

"Is she having medical problems, maybe? Women of a certain age…"

"I don't think she's a certain age yet. She's much younger than the professor."

"Does she know about Ruby? Wait… Is Ruby pregnant?" He shoved a stack of papers at one of the uniforms. "See if Beth Israel will tell you anything. Look under the professor's name and this Ruby. What's her full name?" Detective Hathaway let out a long whistle. "Do you have an address, telephone?"

"Her last name is Quinn. She lives in the grad student apartments on the other side of campus." Jack wrote her phone number and the building address. He knew them by heart, as an expert at calling there looking for his boss and sending flowers, meals, Target deliveries for him. "She must not know about this because she would've come over or called."

"We'll tell her. You can come with us and help us find her if you want."

"Sure."

"We're going to close this office up as a crime scene. Do you need to do anything before you leave, Teddy?"

"No, I'll just go back and do my report. You can lock up with Jack's keys. If you need me, call the school main number."

"Thanks, kid." Detective Engle and Teddy shook hands "So, Jack, you need to leave as well. I need to see everything you take out."

"Sure, just what's in my back-pack. A few student papers, some pens and candy, my calendar, my phone." Jack opened it, neat as a pin. Neither detective looked at individual items in it.

"May I see your phone?"

"Of course."

Detective Hathaway checked the phone's call and message

lists and handed it back. Jack had had no contact with anyone since last evening.

~

Ruby had been out running and was dressed in tattered yoga pants and a Cape Cod t-shirt. Her face was drenched with sweat, and her eyes were red from seemingly unstoppable tears. Someone had stopped her on her run and told her about Morley. Word about the professor was spreading fast around campus.

She looked up as the two detectives came in with Jack. "Jack." She accepted his embrace, still sitting and sobbing uncontrollably. "Jack, what am I going to do?"

"Aw, Ruby. This sucks, I know. I think my head is going to explode." Jack flushed from the uncomfortable feel of Ruby's hug and thought he might faint. He sat on the floor in front of her.

The detectives flashed their badges. "Sorry for your loss but we need to ask you a few questions. We understand that you and the professor were close friends." Detective Hathaway did not pussyfoot around the young woman.

"Yes we were."

"When did you see him last?"

"We had lunch yesterday."

"Did you speak to him after that?"

"No, no I didn't. We had a little tiff and I didn't want to talk to him."

"Tiff?"

"Just stupid things."

"I see. You're getting your master's tomorrow?"

"Yes, I was, but I…"

"What are your plans after that? A little time off? A vacation?"

"No, I have a job in Illinois. I am going to be associate director of curriculum for the South Holland School District.

My master's thesis was a proposal for an integrated American literature curriculum beginning in elementary school and continuing through to high school and AP classes. We are going to implement it over the course of a few years. Very forward-thinking." The more she spoke, the less tears came, and she showed increasing excitement over her new mission.

"You've been here a while, that's a big change. Won't you miss it here?" Detective Hathaway watched her closely.

"Detective, college is a means to an end. I've been working toward this job for six years."

"Was the professor coming with you?"

"The professor? Why would you say that?"

"Well, for one, he has a lot of equity stashed on his own. And he seems to be paying ob/gyn bills, at a time when perhaps his wife is not pregnant."

"I don't know anything about that."

"And you?"

Ruby cupped her round little belly. "Yes, I'm pregnant. Women have families on their own these days." She stood, no longer sobbing, looking indignant.

Hathaway noted the sudden attitude and then continued. "When are you scheduled to go to Illinois?"

"In a few weeks. I don't start work until August."

"Let us know before you go, keep us in the loop if you travel."

"I will."

"Thanks, Miss." The detectives left the lobby, Jack close behind them.

~

JACK PUSHED his phone toward Hathaway to show him Henry Bostick's phone number, who dialed the number on his own phone.

"Mr. Bostick. Detective Hathaway here. Easton Police. We're investigating an incident at Professor Morley's office here at the college. We'd like to ask you a few questions." Jack and Engle heard yelling from the other end of the phone. "Easy, Mr. Bostick. Where are you now? Stay there. We're on our way."

"Want me to come? I know the guy." Jack looked at the two detectives. This time the answer was no.

Jack walked toward the English building, He couldn't get into his office, but he would be able to hang around in the first floor lounge.

~

THE TWO DETECTIVES found Henry at the Student Union. He was sitting on the front steps waiting for them.

"Henry?" Engle held out his hand. "Detective Engle. This is Detective Hathaway." Henry stood.

"Yes?"

"You're a student of Professor Morley?"

"Yeah, I've taken a couple of his classes over the years."

"When was the last time you spoke to him?"

"Yesterday. We had a rather unpleasant meeting."

"Meeting?"

"Yes, he basically took away my job, my doctorate, and my reputation on a pile of baseless accusations."

"You threaten him at all?" Detective Hathaway eyed Henry from head to toe.

"No. I did tell him I would continue to pursue this. For all the good it will do in the next couple of months. This place shuts down tight in summer."

"How well do you know Jack Frye?"

"The TA? If the Professor stops short, Frye's head goes up his ass. Everyone knows that. Frye is as gay as a picnic basket and the talk is that he's in love with his boss. For all the good it will do. Morley has a pretty good-looking wife and an even better-looking girlfriend."

The two detectives looked at each other.

"Henry, are you aware that the professor was found dead in

his office this morning? Someone bashed his head in good and proper," said Detective Engle.

"Wow. It's true, then. I heard it in the student union this morning." Henry sat back down, his right eye twitching.

"We have a witness that heard you threaten the professor yesterday. Don't lie to us, Henry," said Detective Hathaway.

"I didn't lie to you. I never threatened the professor. Never. I told him this wasn't over and it isn't."

"Just what isn't over? Jack Frye said the school did not accept your paper, your work. Why did they do that?"

"I don't know."

"Come on, Jack told us that too. The professor must have files, records of your meetings, of the school's concerns. We can get these documents and things will become clearer." Detective Hathaway reached into his breast pocket for cigarettes that were not there.

"He, the school, the review committee, thinks my research is bogus, that it was taken from just one source, not verified, perhaps even plagiarized. I worked for two years on the research, two years. Came up with nothing. Asked his advice but he was too busy."

"Well, you weren't his only student," said Detective Hathaway.

"Jack told me once that the professor was writing Ruby's master's thesis. The research was something the he had been working on with the intention of writing a book or something. But he drank too much, had Ruby to mess with, had lots of students fawning. He didn't have the chops to finish. But he could parlay it into a nice thesis for his girlfriend."

"Why would he do that?" Detective Engle asked.

"Shrewd. Get her a sizzle topic, lay the whole thing out, get her to present it a few places, and bingo, a school district sees the whole thing and wants her to do it in their schools. As luck would have it, the district is in Illinois. So she takes off with his idea as a lovely parting gift, makes money, gets famous. He gets her out of town before the wife finds out. That girl has a round little stomach that made the rumor mill. Five'll get you ten, that baby's his. Imagine. The deeper in he got, the more he drank. The more he drank, the more he couldn't be bothered with helping me and others. Then when I found out he did her master's paper, I was pissed."

"What did you do?" asked Detective Hathaway.

"I figured he didn't care and so I wrote crap, investigated almost nothing and pumped it up with all the bells and whistles that make literature professors drool—glorious views of ancient manuscripts in little video clips embedded in the thesis, swatches of silk book covers dyed with beet root and other natural dyes, anything the internet had to offer.

"All I needed was for him to weasel word it and work the committee for me. He couldn't even do that. I decided I would go to the committee, confess all my sins, and his. Including the master's thing for Ruby. But I thought I would wait until the fall. The only good thing he gave me was some advice—to go and think about how to proceed. Meanwhile, I have a master's and a bachelor's already so I can teach in Asia or somewhere where they don't check too closely. Those are legitimate degrees. But I'll resent to my dying day his lethargy regarding me and his devotion to his little—"

"Thanks for your candor, Henry. We'll be in touch so stay around or let us know where you are going." Detective Engle gave Henry his card as he and Detective Hathaway walked away from the student union lighting their cigarettes and shaking their heads.

~

The detectives were back at their Easton PD office. They set up a command center in the big conference room, famous for its two white boards and windows that opened. Hathaway drew an elaborate chart on one white board, a sort of organization chart of the professor and the people in his life who might want to harm him.

"Open and shut. This Bostick character had the most to lose." Detective Hathaway chewed on a pen because he wasn't allowed to smoke in the building.

"Really? What about the TA? He had to know what Morley was doing, they shared the same office space. No secrets there. And since Morley drank a lot, I bet he had to clean up a few messes for his boss. Nothing to show for it. Meanwhile Ruby Quinn is having everything handed to her." Detective Engle opened and began eating a yogurt. Detective Hathaway winced.

"So you're saying she did it?"

"Hell no. That would be stupid. She has this guy where she wants him, for better or worse."

"Well, that leaves Jack Frye and Henry Bostick. I still say it's Bostick."

"Too easy."

"Random?" Detective Hathaway was standing at the white board tapping the wet end of his pen onto the names.

"Hell no. What we need is some facts. Fingerprints on the clock or dumbwaiter. Video of the hallway and the comings and goings. A confession.

"Fingerprint discovery is underway. No video in that building. Confession? Wouldn't that be nice." Detective Engle's cell rang.

"Engle. What? On our way." Engle looked over to Hathaway. "Henry Bostick is in the belfry of the condemned school chapel. He has been swinging out the arches and going on about suing the school."

"Drunk?"

"I don't know, but I wish I was," said Detective Engle as he fished out his car keys.

~

BY THE TIME the detectives got to the college, Henry Bostick had tossed his laptop down on the quadrangle, which had been cordoned off with yellow tape by Campus Security Officer

Teddy Sullivan. Bostick also fell off the bell tower, when the wooden slatted floor, put there 100 years ago to make it easier to ring the bells, gave way. He grabbed at the stained glass eyebrow window for support but its rot caused the glass to fall out, taking Henry's wrists with it, cutting them both to bleed madly as he grabbed for the rotten wood frame, which also gave out. It fell to the ground right before Henry. The hospital in Boston told Teddy that he was hanging on by a thread. The thread broke two days later when Henry died of his injuries. The coroner ruled his death a suicide.

~

GRADUATION WENT ON AS PLANNED. Ruby Quinn went to Chicago as scheduled. Professor Morley's wife Caroline went to the Cape alone that summer. Detectives Engle and Hathaway completed their reports, claiming that Henry Bostick killed Professor Morley hours before he plunged to his deliberate death.

Teaching Assistant Jack Frye left a letter of resignation in the first floor faculty mailbox, and went to live in Claremont, New Hampshire, where he hoped to put Professor Morley behind him. The drunken Professor would still be alive if not for catching him skimming from the petty cash that night. It took Frye all night to decide to return the next morning, put on the show like he did for an audience of none and take everything he could. He had a little money now, and a master's thesis ready to publish at one of those online schools that wouldn't give a rat's ass. The only problem he had was the haunting smell of Morley's office that followed him everywhere.

~

May 17th is National Graduation Tassel Day.

BEREFT OF SHAME

BY RANDALL DEWITT

Kerri sat on a stool in the hotel bar, wearing a short cocktail dress, only hours after the day's boring, Into the Light Funeral Conference speeches were over and the evening's excessive partying was well underway. All she had to do was cross her legs a few times, and it wasn't long before she had the attention of the most prominent funeral director there. The "Casket King" bellied up to the bar, introduced himself, and offered to buy her a drink. Despite claiming to have a mortuary cosmetology session early in the morning, Kerri agreed to stay for one more.

"Why are you called the Casket King?" she asked.

"Well, I don't like to brag, but I do more in funeral sales than anyone else in our area."

"Impressive."

"You should see me in action. Getting grief-stricken families who can't afford expensive funerals to purchase our Platinum Package is my specialty." He lifted his brows and made a puppy dog face to demonstrate his sales pitch. "Isn't your dearly departed worth it?"

Kerri listened as the Casket King talked at great length about turning his guilt-tripping sales tactics into a funeral home empire all across New England. By the time they were into a second round of drinks, he'd slipped off his wedding ring and stashed it in his suit jacket pocket. After a few more cocktails, she was dropping her hotel room keycard on the bar and inviting him upstairs for a nightcap.

After pulling back the covers, it wasn't long before Kerri was down to her panties and he, out of his boxer shorts. That's when she disappeared into the bathroom for a moment—returning fully dressed. Kerri pointed to the Wi-Fi streaming, nanny cam alarm clock, strategically placed on the dresser, focused directly on the bed. She watched the blood drain from his face, leaving a complexion so pale, no mortuary cosmetologist could cover.

"I have a Platinum Package that I sell too, except mine's a digital recording." Kerri pouted her lower lip, mimicking his sad, sales pitch face. "Isn't your dear wife worth it to keep her from departing?"

March 11th is National Funeral Director and Mortician Recognition Day.

A BELLOW OF CRIERS

BY LAUREN SHERIDAN

"Janet is such a lovely girl. So accomplished, and you make such a wonderful couple. You really do," Millicent St. John said, tracing a heart into the linen tablecloth with the point of one manicured fingernail. Her steely eyes locked onto Gary Lyons who sat directly across the table from her.

"I think trust is the bedrock of any good relationship, don't you agree?" She leaned forward, the overpowering scent of gardenia reaching out like a lasso round his neck. Her stubby, bejeweled finger returned to the top-right arch of her nail-doodle, and slowly she dragged a jagged diagonal line through the heart, rending it in two.

"What a shame it would be if anything were to jeopardize that trust," she said. Treacle dripped from every word. Leaning back, she resumed her ram-rod straight posture and brought both meaty hands up to her neck to adjust the white ruff that cascaded down her top-heavy bosom.

"Especially now," she said, her voice hard and low—the saccharine-sweet coating melting away to reveal the bitter pill.

And just like that, with two words, the lasso tightened around his neck.

And yet, any passerby overhearing their conversation

would assume that they were just two members of the Town Crier competition enjoying their breakfast in companionable conversation. The competition held on the second Monday of July to coincide with International Town Criers Day was one of the town's summer events. On the day of the event, their oversized white blouses with flowing sleeves tied at the wrists and pirate frills, ornate red coats with gold trim, breeches, knee-high Hessian boots, and tricorn hats might attract the attention of a tourist or two, but would hardly be clocked by the locals.

Their server, a girl that Gary had not seen before and guessed to be in her early twenties, stopped by their table to clear the dishes and drop off the check. She placed the bill presenter diplomatically in the middle of the table. Millicent slid it toward Gary with an exaggerated smile of thanks before picking up the garment bag strewn on the chair next to her in preparation of departing.

"You must be here for the competition," the girl said timidly. "I've never been before. I'm hoping to get out in time to see it." She glanced quickly at the clock before adding, "What exactly is a town crier?"

Millicent's face broke into its most maidenly aunt-like smile, and she nodded at Gary. His throat was dry. He wiped away the sheen of sweat from his brow and cleared his throat before attempting an answer.

"Basically, the town crier was Alexa or Siri in days when most people couldn't read. He was someone who could read and had a strong voice, and he would go to public places and cry out the news, advertisements for local businesses, any new by-laws for the town. Things like that." He finished somewhat lamely.

"Don't forget scandal. One must never forget the juicy, juicy gossip." Millicent winked conspiratorially at the girl.

Then, the older woman's voice became more serious, and she laid a hand on the young girl's arm.

"But I prefer the original name of "bellman" because, of course, he had to grab the townspeople's attention by ringing a bell. Can you guess what the bellman's original role was?" She paused. The girl shook her head.

"He patrolled the streets in the dead of night, arresting ne'er-do-wells, consigning them to the stocks for punishment, and most importantly…" She paused for dramatic effect. "He posted their crimes, so that *everyone* knew what they had done."

She glanced meaningfully at Gary as she rose to leave.

"I will see you in the dressing area just before the competition. You know what to do. I wouldn't be late if I were you."

And with that she turned on her heel, leaving Gary with the bill and a sinking feeling in the pit of his stomach.

Before the old woman had gone a few yards, the server reached under the table and pulled out a rectangular leather box with a sturdy handle. She ran after the bellman holding the black box out in front of her.

"Ma'am, your box."

"Oh, how silly of me. How can I cry out the news without my bell?"

As she said this, her gaze lingered on Gary's face for a moment before she did an about-face and waddled out the door of the restaurant, turning her back on him as he twisted a paper napkin into a noose.

~

THE TINY LAND-LOCKED hamlet of Criersville was located in Central Mass half-way between Worcester and Springfield, the second and third largest cities in Massachusetts. Or as the teenagers of the town described it—half-way between somewhere and nowhere.

Criersville's own professional town crier Godfrey Crowley donned his feathered tricorn hat and assessed the crowd, experiencing a stab of disappointment. It was not a good showing, not compared to the early days when the entire town filled the cobble-stoned main street. Vendors hawking hot dogs, cotton candy, fried dough, and mylar balloons in the shape of town criers used to solicit *his* goodwill to ensure they got the prime real estate—booths closer to the main stage. In those days, Main Street bustled like a traveling circus, and he was its ringmaster.

He sighed at the memory and glanced at the solitary podium and five folding chairs placed in an area just south of the supermarket that provided event parking and whose basement function room supplied the dressing and rest area for the competitors. It was nearly impossible to find vendors for the event these days. Of course, he could always rely on the bank and the local chiropractor, but what he really needed was a celebrity. Someone with a huge social media following. He spent countless hours writing letters and emails, tweeting and posting, to invite actors, politicians, bloggers, and influencers to host the competition, and all he had to show for it were carpal tunnel syndrome and a divorce citing his obsession with town crying as grounds.

A young woman in a pink tank top and shorts sidled up next to Godfrey and giggled while her friend snapped a photo with a cell phone. The pink looked incongruous against the backdrop of the man's scarlet coat adorned in delightfully gaudy, gold buttons and brocade, but there was no denying the Instagram appeal. The girls walked away completely absorbed by the phone's screen, chatting in whispers and bursting out into peals of laughter. Occasionally, they glanced back at him, breaking out into laughter once again.

Of course, Godfrey was used to pausing for a quick selfie with the "punters" as he would refer to them later with undisguised pride in the pub that night before grinning and downing his lager. It was the best night of the year.

"Janet, would you please give the contestants the five-minute warning?" he said to a woman dressed in a modern-day black designer suit in linen and a white cotton shirt. Her brown hair was tied into a French twist, and a pair of emerald-studded sunglasses perched on the bridge of her noise.

He wondered at her choice of clothing on such a warm, summer's day. The criers had no choice. Their layered costumes made the July heat a challenge. Unconsciously, his eye was drawn to a table on his left. Clear glass bottles filled with neon-colored liquid reflected a rainbow of colors onto the white table cloth as the rays of the sun passed through them. As the competition's sponsor, Janet's company Drink Smart had provided complementary beverages to help beat the heat, and she had graciously agreed to be competition dogsbody.

Godfrey suspected Janet Lyons had another reason for volunteering as a grunt for the competition. Her husband Gary was one of this year's finalists. He'd joined the Bellows, the society of town criers, a few years earlier about the time that Sophie Chandler had joined. Quite a few men had joined that year, but Gary had outlasted them all.

Godfrey experienced an unexpected twinge of sympathy for the woman.

"Of course, Godfrey."

"Oh, and don't forget this. Promise me you'll stay hydrated," he said warmly before bending down to reach behind the podium and re-emerging with a bottle of red liquid, which he proffered her. The label sported a town crier holding an oversized bell in mid-ring. The banner at the top read: "A Bellow of Criers". Beneath the crier in a smaller point size was Janet's name. Everyone involved in the event had received a personalized bottle.

"Thank you. I was wondering where that got to."

"No, thank *you*. What a great idea to create a special 'brew' just for today's competition." He raised his hands in inverted commas on *brew*, emphasizing his little joke. From the look on her face, he had misjudged his audience. Well, what did he expect? She had never shown any sense of humor before, why should she surprise him now.

But she did surprise him.

"Well, I wanted to make a special effort as it might be my last." Her voice trailed off distractedly.

"But, s-surely..." he stammered, "for Gary's sake, you'll continue to sponsor the competition."

Before he could finish the thought, she sighed heavily and walked slowly off in the direction of the supermarket.

Godfrey's heart filled with a blackness so pitch, he would have sworn that India ink coursed through his veins.

ENTERING THE SUPERMARKET, Janet broke her stride a bit to enjoy the air-conditioning in the produce aisle before reluctantly walking toward a door tucked discreetly away in the left-hand corner of the adjacent floral department. It opened onto a set of stairs that led to the basement function room the competition used as an ad-hoc rest area.

A sense of dread washed over her as she descended the stairs. *She* would be there.

Her hands tightened on the bottle.

Janet stopped at the bottom of the steps and hesitated, staring at the grey door and breathing in the reassuring remnants of cleaning fluid. The pine-scented chlorine reminded her of the lab. Of the pristine workbench lined with Bunsen burners and test tubes where she had spent her working days just after college. Of being happy. Before she and Gary moved to Criersville. Before he had joined the Bellows. Before *she* had come into their lives and threatened to destroy everything Janet had worked so hard for just when the payoff was in sight.

Acutely aware that she couldn't put it off any longer, she punched the code into the keypad and wrenched open the door.

As Janet entered the room, she scanned it for her husband Gary. In addition to the finalists, a handful of friends and helpers milled about. Two large folding tables had been placed side-by-side in the center of the room. They contained a variety of snacks and bottles of Drink Smart.

Each of the five finalists had been given a folding table with a lighted mirror to help them prep for the competition. Two tables each faced the right-hand wall and back of the room. The wall on the left was shorter than the other two to accommodate the employee restrooms. Accordingly, it only had one table.

It was at that table that she spotted Gary. His movements were furtive. He glanced around his immediate area, and then seemed to be rearranging something on the table. From her position, she could not make out what he was doing with his hands, but when he straightened up, she could see his face in the mirror, and the hatred etched there chilled her to the bone.

The sight had almost made her forget why she was there.

"Five minutes, everyone! Five minutes," she said, projecting her voice into the room with as much authority as she could muster.

She nodded at a couple of the competitors who waved thanks to her. Unwillingly, her eyes searched for Sophie Chandler. The intensity of the desire surprised her. It was like passing a fatal car accident, knowing all you'll find is horror but unable to avert your eyes. She was spared the horror as the young woman was nowhere to be seen, and when she looked back at the station where Gary had been standing, he was no longer there.

Her breath coming faster, she tried to saunter nonchalantly over to the table without attracting attention. A tell-tale prickle heralded the flush that she knew would soon suffuse her face. Why in the world was she over-reacting? After all, her company was the competition's sponsor. She had every right to be there. Still, she fought to regulate her breathing.

A variety of items occupied the table that Gary had been searching. They included all the items one might expect, such as an opened eye-shadow palette, tube of lipstick, a hair brush, tissues, a jar of cold cream, some cotton swabs, and a leather case containing a gold-plated bell. There was also something unexpected. Next to the case, stood a very beautiful, cut-glass atomizer filled with a light-amber liquid. The black leather provided the perfect backdrop. A top fashion photographer could not have set the scene better, with the gleaming brass nestled in the case's red velvet lining encased by the smooth black leather, which in turn, made the atomizer pop.

Janet leaned forward, put her bottle down, and reached out for the atomizer.

"Ah, I see you have found my pride and joy," said a crisp, sharp voice behind her.

She jumped.

"My dear, I'm so sorry. I startled you."

Millicent St. John, her face showing exaggerated concern, placed a meaty hand on Janet's arm. Reflexively, she pulled away and then blushed.

The older woman smiled. She placed the personalized Drink Smart bottle she was carrying on the table before pulling out the chair and sitting down. She picked up the atomizer and turned it, so that the angled cuts in the glass caught the light.

Then, she brought it close to her lips, opened her mouth wide, and sprayed the contents of the atomizer into the back of her mouth. Janet gasped.

"You thought it was perfume, didn't you?"

As if on cue, a ripple of a cloying floral scent assaulted Janet's nostrils. Something else cut through the scent. Something that opened her sinus passages wide.

"It's a family heirloom passed down from my great grand-mama." Millicent said coyly. "An opera singer's atomizer."

Janet examined the atomizer more closely and realized that its nozzle tube was longer than a normal perfume atomizer, presumably to spray all the way to the back of the throat.

"What's inside it?" she asked.

"It's my own, particular concoction of saline, honey, eucalyptus and, of course, vodka. It works wonders to soothe the vocal cords."

Her eyes glinted with mischief.

"You're not the only brewer of magical elixirs in town, you know," she said, raising her own personalized Drink Smart bottle in a mock toast.

"But you are the most successful, I'll grant you that."

Janet shifted uncomfortably.

"Oh, dear. Surely, you didn't think your golden goose was a secret. Or should I say parachute. I believe that's what they call it, don't they? It is a small town, my dear. Everyone knows everyone's business. You're quite a Cinderella Story, aren't you? And your fairy godmother has been very, very busy, I see."

Her eyes combed over Janet as if considering the purchase of livestock, appraising her designer apparel, expensive shoes, and the custom sunglasses perched on her head with tiny emeralds shaped in a monogram of JL on the stems.

Janet flushed as if she were a young child trying on her mother's clothes and make-up, who is greeted by patronizing smiles and suppressed laughter when proudly showing off the results. She just wanted her husband to see what their future could be like if they could just hold on a little longer.

"But…" Millicent elongated the word for effect, "I imagine that, in some ways, you might be a bit of a reverse Cinderella Story. I wonder…"

"Wonder what?" Janet's voice was harsh.

"Well, my dear, I wonder if Cinderella became rich in her own right, if she might not, well, lose Prince Charming?"

The old woman patted Janet's left arm with her free hand and gave her a pitying look.

"You know what men are."

The words slapped Janet in the face. Her skin burned under the terrible heat of the crier's hand. Without thinking, she wrenched her arm away and in the violence of doing so, she connected with Millicent's Drink Smart bottle. It flew out of the old woman's hand, hung suspended in the air momentarily before its rapid descent and shattering impact.

Millicent turned to look at the pools of purple liquid and chards of glass. When she faced Janet again, her face was flush with excitement, indescribable pleasure flooded her face.

"Butterfingers. I'm sure you won't mind if I take your bottle, will you dear. I am so parched."

Janet remained dazed and immovable while Millicent called

out cheerily to the others that they had better get a move on. She closed the lid of her bell box, put her atomizer and Janet's Drink Smart into her reticule, and prepared to leave.

As she followed the other criers out of the room, she called over her shoulder.

"You'll mop that up, won't you, dear."

~

GODFREY GLANCED AT HIS WRISTWATCH. Off to a late start. The crowd of twenty or so family, friends, and tourists sat in folding chairs facing the podium. No one seemed particularly anxious, but he was a professional. He had standards. The competition may be under attack, but he wasn't going down without a fight.

Just as he was about to delegate someone to go see what was holding up the competitors, Gary Lyons and Sophie Chandler appeared, somewhat surprisingly from his right, the opposite direction from the supermarket parking lot. As they rounded the corner, Gary grabbed Sophie's arm, pulling her close. He wore a tense expression, and Sophie's cheeks and eyes shone bright.

Snippets of their conversation reached Godfrey's ears.

"What does it matter? Whether it is now or later." Sophie's clear voice cut across the ambient noise.

The chatter of a group of middle-aged women debating the merits of a gluten-free diet drown out Gary's reply.

"I don't care about the money," the young woman responded.

"You will when you're my age," said Gary.

"I won't wait forever," said Sophie, pulling away from him before they took their seats on the folding chairs to the right of the podium in silence. Once again, Godfrey experienced a surprising prick of sympathy for Janet Lyons.

Within minutes, Millicent St. John arrived with the final two competitors in tow. She promenaded regally in front of the podium, nodding and smiling greetings to the crowd. Her hooped skirt, twirled as she completed a wide circuit to her seat.

Regally, she inclined her head toward Godfrey as if giving him permission to start.

Of all the nerve. Who was in charge of this competition anyway? Not the sponsor and certainly not Ms. Millicent St. John. Godfrey Crowley was the official town crier of Criersville, and he would perform his duties as he saw fit to the last.

"Ladies and Gentlemen, thank you for coming to 25th Annual Town Criers Competition," he said into the microphone after giving the preliminary remarks regarding recordings and flash photography.

"In today's competition, five finalists will be crying out a news story of their own creation. They will be judged on how well they grab your attention, the precision of their wording, and the dignity of their comportment. But finally, they will be judged on their ability to sustain a loud volume throughout their speech. And you, ladies and gentleman, shall be their judges."

The crowd clapped. He removed the mic from its holder and held it out toward the audience.

"You call that loud? You know what the collective noun is for a group of criers? It's a bellow—a bellow of criers. So, let's try it again with a real bellow this time!"

The crowd managed to produce some "Woo, woo" sounds. Enough to satisfy Godfrey.

"And now without further ado, I give you our first finalist Millicent St. John."

After taking one final spray from the atomizer, Millicent cleared her throat and placed the atomizer on the ground. Opening the drawstring of her reticule, she extracted her scroll and picked up her bell. Godfrey groaned inwardly and glanced none too surreptitiously at his watch. Trust Millicent to eke out her entrance like some C-list actress prolonging her death scene.

As she rose, her round face was flushed, and sweat glistened on her forehead. Her gait appeared rather unsteady as she stepped forward.

With her left hand, she lifted her bell and then let the momentum do the rest. The clanging sound rang out crisp and clear through the summer air. She opened her mouth as if to cry out the opening "Hear ye, hear ye" when she suddenly teetered forward and collapsed into a silent heap.

Godfrey stood paralyzed. All color had drained from his face. As one, the spectators leaned forward, but no one moved. Gary launched out of his chair, practically pushing Sophie over to be the first person to reach the stricken woman's side. He leaned in to check her breath. His fingers nervously rummaged through layers of costume. Seconds ticked by before he managed to extract an arm and check for a pulse. But even before he spoke, Godfrey knew what the other man would say.

"She's dead."

"SHERIFF, do you mind telling us exactly why in God's name you want to see us here?" said Godfrey. He spread his hands wide to indicate the supermarket's basement function room.

"As you can imagine, we are extremely upset at the loss of one of our members. What possible help can we give you? With the exception of Sophie, none of us are medical experts."

Sheriff Ray Miller assessed his suspects. Godfrey Crowley sat with his arms crossed in a folding chair on the far-right. He had removed his coat and other crier accessories, and loosened the top buttons of his shirt. Next to him was Sophie Chandler who worked as a nurse at the Criersville Clinic. Ray took a moment to appreciate the form-fitting version of the crier's costume that she wore. It was tailored in the waist and hips to cling to the curves of her body. And she had curves. On her left sat Gary Lyons, a pharmaceutical company rep. From all reports, he made sure that he was the first to reach the woman after she collapsed. Now, his face showed all the exhaustion of a marathon runner without any of the exhilaration. And finally, Janet Lyons sat on the far-left, her folding chair a good three feet from her husband's. Her eyes wary. Her lips tight.

One of these four people killed Millicent St. John.

"Well, Mr. Godfrey, we have confirmed that the victim died of cyanide poisoning," Ray said.

"What?" said Sophie. "That's not possible."

She turned to look at Gary and slid back on her chair slightly closer to Godfrey. *Curious.*

"Not possible? Why is that Ms. Chandler?"

"I mean…" She blushed. "Who would want to kill Millicent?"

Janet's gaze shifted to Gary. Gary turned toward Sophie. Godfrey scowled at Janet.

Curiouser and curiouser.

"It could have been an accident, couldn't it?" Janet said. A mixture of urgency and hope tinged her voice.

"No, Mrs. Lyons. It couldn't."

Ray paused for a moment and surveyed each one of them in turn.

He pointed to an object on the table standing between him and the suspects. They leaned forward.

"That's Millicent's scroll," said Gary. His voice was strained.

"Yes, it is. Do you notice anything out of the ordinary about it?"

Gary and the others came over to the table to examine the scroll.

"Please, don't touch it."

The group ran their eyes over every detail of the scroll, which was rolled out to reveal Millicent's news. Ray remained silent as they scanned the text quickly. He watched for their reactions.

Janet Lyons grew pale, Godfrey flushed red, Gary grew wary, and Sophie grabbed the brass ring.

"Look!" she cried. "There's more paper curled up at the top."

She pointed to the wooden dowel on which the scroll was wrapped. Clearly visible was another sheet, slightly uncurling from the dowel.

"What is it?" she said.

"Apparently, Millicent had a little side business. Although, I suspect that one, or two, of you are already aware of that." Ray's eyes lingered on Gary and Sophie for a moment. Sophie flushed crimson.

"I suspect she hid another version of her 'news' for the competition just in case."

"Just in case what?" demanded Godfrey.

"In case, her blackmail victim decided not to pay up, which is exactly what we first suspected. But the funny thing is... they did."

"Did what?" Godfrey spat out.

"Paid up. We found 5,000 dollars in the lining of Ms. St. John's bell box. We also have a witness who says that you were standing at Ms. St. John's station earlier, Mr. Lyons. What exactly were you doing there?"

Anger flashed across Gary's face.

"I just wanted to wish Millicent good luck. You know, a let-the-best-crier-win kind of thing."

"Well, if that is all it was, perhaps, we should just read the hidden scroll."

Ray made forward as if to pick up the scroll. Gary appeared to be on the verge of exploding, but before he could say a word, Janet Lyons spoke for the first time since Ray had entered the room.

"I did it. I killed Millicent St. John. I poisoned her atomizer."

There was a stunned silence.

"Why did you do that, Mrs. Lyons?" Ray said.

"You don't know what it was like. That woman was horrible. Always spying. Watching your every move. The puppet master, and everyone in town her own little puppets, especially the criers. She reveled in every twisted minute of it."

Tears filled her eyes.

"It's insidious. That's one of the reasons why I'm withdrawing sponsorship of the competition and have been lobbying the town meeting members to eliminate the position of town crier, get rid of the competition altogether, and focus on other ways to promote tourism."

"And the other reason?" Ray asked.

She turned to Gary.

"I just thought if you didn't have the town criers. We might find a way back to where we used to be… no matter what you had done."

If she were looking for comfort, she didn't get it. Gary stepped closer to Sophie, who placed a hand on his arm. A stunned Janet collapsed back onto her seat.

Godfrey Crowley's face betrayed utter disbelief.

"Penny for your thoughts, Mr. Crowley," said Ray.

"Huh, what?"

"Well, this is pretty dramatic stuff. What are your thoughts?"

"I don't know what you mean," he said indignantly.

"Not even if I tell you that the atomizer contained no trace of poison."

"But Janet. She confessed."

Ray smiled at Janet.

"I think we all know why she did that."

"No, the poison was in the red Drink Smart bottle with Janet's name on it."

"What?" Janet exclaimed. "But that bottle never left my sight after Godfrey handed it to me."

In seconds, her expression transformed from puzzled to enraged.

"You bastard!" She lunged at Godfrey. "You tried to kill me."

The propulsion of the unforeseen attack brought them both crashing to the floor. Ray rushed over to haul Janet off of Godfrey. The older man sprawled on the floor with a dazed countenance.

"Why?" Janet said in a strangled voice.

"It was self-defense. You were taking everything from me —the competition, the Bellows, my whole life. I had no choice."

Ray nodded to two officers standing in the back, who came forward and escorted Godfrey out of the room.

On his way out, he muttered, "You know it's funny. You can get anything online these days, not just the news.

~

The second Monday in July is International Town Criers Day.

BLACK FRIDAY BLUES

BY CAROL KAUFMAN

I woke up in a hospital bed to a throbbing head and double vision, with no idea how I had gotten there. Through the haze I saw a blob of figures floating around the foot of the bed. When I groaned, the figures turned toward me. One of them, I assume a doctor, told me I had been carjacked and that I had suffered some pretty bad injuries. I would be their "guest" for a couple of days.

I fell back asleep.

By the next day, the double vision had gone, but traces of the headache remained. A tall police detective with a mop of silver-threaded black hair came to visit. He introduced himself as Detective Sergeant Rogers. He and my husband Eric shook hands before getting down to business. The detective asked all the questions a binge-watcher of *Law and Order* would expect him to ask. Too bad I couldn't remember a thing about the "incident."

"As you recover, maybe something will come back to you," he said.

I gulped. "Why would somebody be after me? I'm a yoga teacher. I don't have lots of money. And look at the lame car he took. A ten-year-old Taurus. Hardly a gem."

"Don't jump to conclusions. This probably has nothing to

do with you," Eric said. "And remember, you were a woman alone at night."

"Exactly. There's been a series of these incidents over the past month. So try not to obsess," Detective Rogers said.

Easy for you to say.

"You'll just make yourself sick." He had kind eyes the color of sea glass. They were comforting.

Eric put his hand on mine. "She's had a tough go. I think she needs to rest."

The detective pulled a business card from his pocket and handed it to Eric, who smiled.

"Gorham Rogers? Do your friends call you Silver?"

Rogers groaned. "Hi ho."

Eric did a double-take "Wait a minute. This says you're with the major cases squad."

I bolted upright, making the room spin. *What?*

"Yes, I'm afraid one of the carjackings ended in a death. That's why I'm on the case."

Oh my God. I am so lucky to be alive. I sank back onto the pillow, my head pounding like a jackhammer.

The detective took out another card. "I'm writing my personal cell phone number here in case you think of something off-hours. Don't be shy about calling. I want to catch this guy as much as you do."

He handed this second card to me.

"Thank you, Detective."

He stood to leave. "I'll stop by your house when you're feeling better. Maybe you'll remember something by then. And have a good Thanksgiving."

Thanksgiving! I'd totally forgotten about that.

I WAS THRILLED to be back in my own home but didn't have the energy to do anything for myself. Eric unpacked my bag while I sat down on the edge of the bed to undress.

"The doctors said your body will heal with time but that you might have some PTSD from the trauma. They said you should consider seeing a counselor."

I grunted. *There was no way I was going out of the house. Maybe ever. If a shrink wanted to see me, it'd have to be here or online.*

"Oh, and Meg from the yoga studio called to see how you were."

I haven't even thought of the studio.

"I'll just have to cancel my classes or find somebody to take over for me."

"It's all taken care of, babe. Don't worry yourself. I'm here for you."

I lifted the covers and got into bed, lowering my head slowly to avoid aggravating the tender spots. The cool, soft-as-silk sheets felt so much better against my skin than the stiff hospital linens.

Thanksgiving! "I've got to talk to Sally about doing Thanksgiving dinner here."

"And screw up her sacrosanct rotation system? You know how your sister is about that."

"I think she'll give me a break this year, Eric."

"How about some tea?" he asked.

Eric was being so solicitous I could cry. Such a sweetheart.

"Sure. Thanks."

Exhaustion swept over me and I closed my eyes. When I opened them, the teacup was sitting on the nightstand next to me. The brew was cold.

That night we ate scrambled eggs and toast at the kitchen counter. If I didn't know better, it would have looked for all the world like a typical Wednesday evening.

~

AT 6 A.M. THE next day, my best friend Jen was at the back door with a shopping bag filled with my favorite blueberry scones and a pile of magazines. And big, but gentle, hugs.

"How're you doing, kid?" she asked as she dumped everything out onto the kitchen counter. "Did you sleep okay?"

I shrugged. "Not great. I had nightmares."

"I guess that's normal, right? What did they say at the hospital?"

"They recommended counseling."

Eric, still clad in his standard t-shirt and boxers that worked as pajamas, popped his head through the kitchen door.

"Hey, Jen."

"Hey Eric, why don't you go for your run? I'll stay here with Andi."

Just like Jen. Always thinking of others. She knew Eric would probably go bonkers if he couldn't have his daily workout. His schedule was set in stone: 5:30 a.m. running, then weights at the gym. Taking care of me had really made a mess of his to-do list.

Eric crossed the kitchen and planted a kiss on my head, then went to change into his running gear.

Jen poured us both coffee and buttered two scones. She set two plates on the reclaimed oak farm table and sat down across from me. The steam from the mugs carried a heavenly aroma of hazelnut.

"Have the police found the guy who did this?" she asked.

Right to the point, Jen. "Not yet, but they did find the car."

"How does it look?"

"Eric says it's okay. I haven't been outside to look at it."

Jen's eyebrows went up.

We sipped in silence for a couple of minutes when a sudden panic attack shoved me out of my chair. I paced around the kitchen, my heart racing in my chest. Sweat broke out on my upper lip and I began to hyperventilate.

Jen's face went pale. I must have looked like a lunatic. Jen jumped up and put her arms around me.

"What's the matter?" she asked.

"What am I going to do when Eric goes back to work tomorrow?" My whole body was shaking.

"What're you afraid of?"

"What if the guy was really after me? The detective said there's been a series of carjackings. What if this guy was really after me and he did the other ones just to throw the police off the track?"

"Andi, slow down. You've been watching way too much TV. You need to chill."

She led me back to my chair. I sat down and began my pranayama breathing. *Some role model I am for a yoga teacher.*

"Maybe you can install an alarm system. Would that make you feel better?" she asked.

"I'm not sure we can afford one."

"There are good systems out there that don't cost an arm and a leg. Let's talk with Eric when he gets back."

I nodded. "That's a good idea." Just the thought of an alarm made my breathing slow and the cramp in my stomach relax.

"We're here for you. You'll feel better soon."

I stood up. "I'm going back to bed."

Jen scooped up the magazines and offered them to me.

"Maybe later. I'm tired now." We hugged and I turned and went upstairs.

~

Jen came back the next morning and dove right into business. "Will Meg save your place at the yoga studio?"

"She said she would, but I'm not sure I ever want to go back, Jen. Being in that parking lot would totally freak me out."

Can't she see I can never go back to the place where some violent psychopath beat me up and stole my car?

Jen squinted at me. "So, what are you going to do for a living if you don't leave the house?"

Jen had a point. What was I going to do?

I changed the subject. "Your birthday is coming up. What do you want to do to celebrate?"

"Let's go out to lunch. It'll do you good to get out."

"Uh, no. Why don't you come over here? I'll make lunch."

Jen sighed. I could see the wheels turning in her head. She would put up with my craziness for a while, but not for too long. We made a date for lunch and she left. I gathered up the magazines from the counter where Jen had left them and headed upstairs.

Back in bed, I flipped through the magazines, not really focusing on anything. Until I came to an article about celebrity cake decorators. The photos of their creations were tantalizing. And that's when the idea came to me. There was no way I'd go out to a restaurant, but I could make Jen a really special lunch right here. I'd make one of these cakes for her birthday. Even though I knew nothing about cake decorating, I chose a basket weave design overflowing with flowers in pink and lavender, her favorite colors.

I fell asleep with the magazine open on my chest, thinking about online ordering.

~

THE ALARM SYSTEM was installed the following Tuesday, and my soreness had eased enough that I could get up and start doing things around the house. I had organized everything online, ordering groceries, cleaning supplies, books, gifts, postage stamps, and cake decorating supplies. There would never be a need to go outside again.

We tried to keep as normal a routine as possible. Eric got up and went for his workout every morning before work. I did my own yoga routine in the house. The rest of my days I practiced baking cakes and piping buttercream flowers.

"How about a movie tonight?" Eric asked that night after work.

"I'll check Netflix."

"No. I meant go out to an actual theater. Or dinner. Or a club. You're a great dancer."

"I'm not ready yet."

"Andi, I love you. You need to get out of this house."

My face grew hot. "Weren't you the one who said it might take some time?"

"I also said you could use some counseling. You can't just spend the rest of your life in the house watching TV and drinking tea."

"I don't need counseling. When they catch the bastard and put him away, I'll feel better."

Eric moved to put his arms around me.

Or am I falling apart?

"Andi, this is absolutely amazing," Jen said. "Lunch was great, but this…" She spun the finished cake on its turntable that sat on the counter. She examined every rose and leaf.

"Thanks. I actually enjoyed doing it. It required focus, which kept my mind off my troubles."

Jen sat down at the kitchen table. She pulled on her earlobe, a sure sign she was cooking up something, so I wasn't surprised when she jumped up from her chair.

"Andi! Why don't you start a cake decorating business?"

"You're crazy. I've made one cake. That's not a business."

"So, you'll start small and grow. Your work is so good you'll have lots of customers."

"I don't know, Jen."

Jen paused for a dramatic *coup de grace*. "And you can do it in the house."

Hmm. That part actually sounded attractive. Ordering online is the best. Except.

"I don't want strangers in the house."

"So, you can take orders online." Jen's face was flushed and her eyes were gleaming. She was really getting into this.

Where did this girl get her energy?

"But how are people going to know about me?" I asked.

"We'll start with fliers and post them around town. Then

we'll make a website and post pictures of your cakes. And I'll tell everybody I come in contact with."

This might actually work.

Jen continued describing her grandiose plan. "Of course, that means you'll have to make a few cakes to display, but that can be just until you have actual customers."

I mulled it over. "Abby's birthday is next week. I suppose I could make a cake for her."

"Yes! A cake from her auntie will be so much better than one from the bakery."

"They're pros, Jen. I'm not."

"But you will be, Andi. I can feel it."

"Next week is kind of fast. I just learned how to do flowers."

Jen gave me the stink-eye. "What else are you doing in the house all day? Watching soap operas and game shows?"

She sounds just like Eric.

I sighed. "Okay, okay. I'll do one for Abby. She loves *The Secret Garden*. Maybe I can do something with that. And it'll give me a chance to practice my flowers."

"And Eric's birthday is next month, so do one for him, too."

I sank back into my chair. *No sense arguing with Jen. She's a force of nature. And working from home does sound good.*

"Okay, but first I have to cook the turkey."

~

THE FAMILY HAD INDULGED me by coming to our house for Thanksgiving, but my sister Sally had made it very clear that she wouldn't tolerate my "madness" much longer. I managed to get through the day okay and even found myself laughing more than once. My brother Danny did some magic tricks and Abby played the piano. I guess having everybody I loved around me took my mind off the attack.

I was up before the crack of dawn on Black Friday, the house still smelling of sage stuffing and caramelized onions. Once Eric left for his run, I sat down at the computer with my

Christmas list, once again thanking the internet gods for online ordering. Less than an hour later, I was done. If I forgot anything, there was still Cyber Monday to finish up.

That task checked off my to-do list, I enjoyed my favorite post-Thanksgiving breakfast of leftover pumpkin pie and pumpkin spice coffee. Just as I took my first bite of the pie, the doorbell rang. I panicked. *Who could possibly be coming to the house at this hour?* My heart pounding, I tiptoed through the kitchen to the living room and, with damp hands, pushed aside the curtain on the window overlooking the front yard.

Our neighbor from down the road, Jeff, was standing at the front door. *What was he doing here? Why did Eric have to be on his run now?* I got down on the floor, praying that he hadn't seen me peeking through the window.

Jeff rang the bell a second time After what seemed like an hour but was probably only a minute, I got up and went to the door. There, on the doormat, was the morning *Times*. It must have been delivered to Jeff's house by mistake. Feeling like a fool, but with my heart still racing, I picked it up.

After I calmed down, I turned to work on Abby's birthday cake. My niece loved anything purple, so I colored the buttercream frosting icing in several shades, plus some pink and yellow for contrast. I practiced my piping, getting better with each flower.

If do say so myself, this Secret Garden cake is going to look great.

I stood to stretch, interlacing my fingers behind my back and lifting my arms. The oven going full blast with a practice cake had me sweating, so I wandered onto the screen porch. The November day was unseasonably warm, and the air was clean and refreshing.

I watched squirrels darting along the bare branches of our towering oak tree and a lonely cardinal hopping across the lawn. Spruce and fir provided the only green in the yard, but red holly berries added some cheer.

Could somebody break through our screens and get into the house?

I raised my eyes to scan the neighborhood. Houses were

staggered along the streets in this neighborhood, separated from each other by a stream that ran through a swath of conservation land, so the only house I could see full-on was on the far side of the of the stream. Like ours, the windows were open to the beautiful day.

Maybe when Eric gets home from his run, we'll go outside together.

I lowered myself into my Nana's old wicker chair. This chair and its comfy floral cushions had always been my happy place, bringing up memories of summers on the lake. When Nana died, no one in the family argued when I said I wanted it.

Loud, angry voices penetrated my consciousness, pulling me out of the chair. My eyes swept the area to locate the source. I squinted and saw through the windows of the house across the way what looked like two people struggling. I was surprised by how far the voices carried, and they were getting louder and angrier.

Then a door slammed, and everything went silent. I ran to the den to find our binoculars, but by the time I got back to the porch and adjusted the focus, all I could see was a car backing out of the attached garage. I grabbed my phone to call Jen.

"It really sounded bad, Jen. I think something terrible may have happened."

"Calm down, Andi," she said. "It was probably just a typical couple's fight. Don't you and Eric ever argue? Remember, you're still jumpy from the carjacking. Don't get irrational."

Was I being irrational?

We hung up and I went back to the kitchen. My mouth was dry so I went to the fridge to get something to drink. The water pitcher was slick with condensation, so I used both hands to grip it. I shut the fridge door with my foot, but slammed it so hard that I jumped, almost dropping the pitcher.

That terrible night flashed back, the car door slamming and my head hitting the pavement. I froze in place, my heart racing and my head going light. I did some deep breathing for a full minute before I was able to complete my task.

Jen's right. I've got to calm down. I'm making myself crazy.

I went back to putting the finishing touches on Abby's cake, making sure that every tree, shrub, bird, and flower went to its right spot. I inspected my handiwork one last time before I'd hand it over to Eric's sister, Liv. Feeling pretty good about my progress as a cake decorator and businesswoman, I poured myself a cup of coffee, sat down at the table, and picked up the newspaper.

Just as I finished reading the editorial, Eric returned from his run, flushed and sweating. Holding his balled-up t-shirt under one arm, he went to the fridge and refilled his water bottle.

"Look at you, you're drenched."

"It's weirdly warm out there today. I wasn't dressed for it, so I had to slow down to rest a few times. I'm gonna go grab a shower. I'll throw this stuff in a wash while I'm at it," he said, pointing to his running clothes.

"Eric, I saw something disturbing across the way."

He raised an eyebrow. "Yeah? What'd you see?"

I told him about the two people fighting, the loud voices, and the slammed door.

Eric leaned against the doorjamb. "Babe, it's really none of our business. But if it'll make you feel better, we can call the police."

What would I tell them? Officer, I heard a couple fighting?

I sighed. "You're probably right. I just happened to hear them because the windows were open."

"Right. You don't want to get irrational."

Irrational? Are Eric and Jen talking to each other?

I shrugged. "Go take your shower. You really stink."

Eric laughed.

~

VOICES RISING from the living room woke me at around 8 o'clock the following Tuesday morning. I still groaned like an old lady, but I managed to get up, throw on a pair of jeans and a t-shirt, and go downstairs. Detective Rogers was in the living room with Eric.

"How are you feeling, Ms. Steele?" Rogers asked, unfolding himself from his seat on the sofa.

"I'm okay. Thank you."

"Mr. Boniface tells me you're not leaving the house."

"That's right. There's no need. I can do everything from here. I can even order postage stamps online."

Rogers coughed. "Then I'm glad to bring some good news. We got lucky with surveillance video of your carjacker. It was pretty blurry, but our tech guys are trying to clean it up now. I think we'll be making an arrest very soon."

"That's wonderful news. Thank you for letting us know," Eric said.

"So now you can go outside without a worry," Rogers said.

What? "Uh, no. Not yet."

"We'll get her out soon, Detective," Eric said. "She just needs to rest a bit longer."

I crossed the room and sat down on the loveseat. "Detective Rogers, did Eric tell you about what I saw?"

Eric shot me a look of horror. *He thinks I'm losing my mind.*

Rogers frowned. "What did you see?"

"Eric thinks I'm overreacting to a fight I heard. But there was shouting and door slamming, so loud I could hear it from hundreds of yards away."

Eric got up from his seat and took the spot next to me. He put his arm around my shoulders.

"Detective Rogers, Andi saw their car back out of the driveway, so everything must be cool." Eric turned to me. "Listen, I've gotta get ready for work. Thanks for stopping by, Detective."

The two men stood and shook hands, and Eric headed upstairs.

Rogers sat down again. "So, how are you—really?"

"Eric thinks I'm hallucinating. Did you see the look on his face when I mentioned the neighbors' fight?"

Rogers shrugged. "I did. He's being very protective of you."

"I'm afraid he's losing patience with me. He's tired of staying home, and he really isn't happy about having to do the laundry. My back is still too sore to lift it."

Rogers grimaced. "That was one my ex-wife's biggest complaints about me. I did the laundry. Not well."

Despite myself, I laughed.

He stood to leave. "I'll drop in again. You take care. And if you need anything, please call."

"Thank you, Detective."

~

JEN CALLED ON SUNDAY AFTERNOON, and the phone line practically buzzed with her energy. "Hey, Andi. Pete and I just got home from Canada. The fishing was great and I'll fill you in when I see you tomorrow. Anyway, I just found an email from a potential customer. A woman I'm friendly with from my Pilates class saw the flier I posted at the gym, and she copied your email address. But she wrote it down wrong, so her message bounced back.

"Anyway, she sent it over a week ago, so you should really get right back to her. I've forwarded it to you and I let her know about the delay."

"Wow. Thanks, Jen. That's the third order this week. How many fliers did you put up?"

"A bunch. And you'll get more once we've got your website up and running so people can order, and pay you, directly."

"I hope I'll be able to keep up with what I've already got."

I went to my laptop and found the email Jen had forwarded. It was from a woman named Petra Rooney who wanted a "very special" cake for her engagement party. Attached were a couple of photos with milestone events that she wanted depicted on the cake.

I clicked on the first icon. It was a jpeg image of the running path by the river. It was a pretty place lined with flowering shrubs, leafy trees, and benches. Eric and I liked to go biking there.

At least, we did.

Then I clicked on the second icon. And there was a selfie of the woman I assume was Petra Rooney. With Eric. They were both in running clothes. With their arms around each other, smiling.

I called Jen. The second she picked up, I shouted at her. "Did you look at these pictures?"

"Andi, calm down. What pictures are you talking about?"

"Stop telling me to calm down."

"Okay. Just tell me what you're so upset about."

"Did you look at the email you forwarded to me? Did you look at the attachments?"

"I read the message, sure. That's how I knew it was for you. But I certainly didn't open the attachments. Let me finish with my client and I'll be right over."

I got up and began to pace around the house.

~

WITH JEN BY MY SIDE, I picked up the phone to dial Petra Rooney and give her a piece of my mind. A man answered the phone.

She's having an affair with my husband and she's married?

"I'd like to speak with Petra, please," I said, my pulse pounding in my ears.

"Who's calling, please?"

"This is Andi Steele. She sent me an order for a custom cake."

A slight hesitation on the other end, then a cough. "Ms. Steele, this is Detective Rogers."

What? "Why are you answering her phone?"

"I'm here on a wellbeing check. I'm afraid Ms. Rooney is missing."

I think my heart actually stopped for a second.

"Oh my God. What happened?"

"Why don't I come over when I'm done here? I'm right around the corner."

~

Detective Rogers settled into a kitchen chair and launched right into interview mode.

"Tell me again why you were calling Ms. Rooney at home."

I repeated what Jen had said about the email address and the cake order and her camping trip.

Rogers jotted down my answers in a little notebook. His head was down, so I couldn't see what was in his eyes.

Does he suspect me of something? I just found out about the two of them.

"Ms. Rooney told co-workers that she was going to the Maritime Provinces with her boyfriend, and that she expected him to propose while they were there."

Her boyfriend? Propose? I was trying to maintain control, but my heart galloped.

"When she didn't show up for work this morning, her manager tried to reach her. She didn't answer, so he called 911. The next-door neighbor let us into the house. Nobody was there."

"Did she go to the Maritimes?" I asked.

"The resort manager says she never showed up."

The detective made another note. *Had I said something important?*

"What about her car?" I asked.

"It's in her garage."

Rogers checked his notes. "You and your husband have different last names."

Change of subjects?

"That's right."

Then Rogers sat up as if somebody had jolted him with an electric cattle prod.

"Remember that fight you told me about? The one that had you so worried?"

"Of course, I do."

"Which house was that?"

I stood up and headed to the screen porch. He followed. When I pointed it out, he sighed.

"Ms. Steele, that's Petra's Rooney's house. You didn't know her?"

"I only knew that somebody had recently moved in, but I hadn't met them."

"We found a photo of your husband in her bedroom."

Light-headed, I sank into Nana's wicker chair and put my head between my knees, praying for some comfort. But this time the chair wasn't giving me any.

A sudden thought made me grasp the chair arms and lean forward.

"Detective, do you remember that day when I first told you about the fight?"

"Uh huh."

"Eric said not to obsess about it because I had seen the car back out of the driveway, so everything was cool."

"And?"

I took a deep, shaky breath. "I never told him about the car."

Rogers pulled up a chair.

"I know it'll be hard to remember something that happened so long ago, but do you happen to recall what he was wearing the day of that fight?"

I closed my eyes, trying to bring back that day.

It was warm outside. The windows were open. He came home drenched with sweat.

My eyelids flew open. "He took his shirt off and then did a load of laundry."

"Can you find his running clothes from that day?"

"Why?" My stomach began to churn.

"We found blood spatter in the kitchen. Some was wiped up. We need to see if there's any on his clothing."

"But he did the laundry."

"We can still find traces of blood, even after washing."

Detective Rogers' kind, green eyes looked sad. "Ms. Steele, I am so sorry, but we're going to have to take your husband in for questioning."

The house closed in on me. It felt dirty. For the first time since the carjacking, I wanted to go outside and breathe fresh air.

"Do you have one of those two-way mirrors?" I asked. "I want to hear what he has to say. And I want to see his face when he says it."

"You can ride with me." He went to the front door and opened it. I froze and I felt the blood drain from my head. Detective Rogers helped me to a chair.

"I'll be with you the whole time. Nobody will hurt you."

I nodded and managed to stand up without falling down.

~

"How did the affair start?" Detective Rogers asked.

Eric drummed his fingers on the table in the tiny interrogation room.

How are you going to rationalize this, Eric?

"I met Petra on her regular morning run on the river walk. She was a beautiful woman in a sexy running outfit. We talked and laughed."

"Your wife is a beautiful woman," Rogers said.

"Andi was in the damned house all day long. It was like she just gave up after the carjacking. But Petra was exciting to be with. What was I supposed to do? Live like a monk?" His face was red and the vein in his forehead was pulsing.

"The carjacking only took place a few weeks ago. How long had you been seeing Ms. Rooney?"

"Only a few weeks."

You pig.

Rogers continued his questioning. "And you led Petra to believe your marriage was on the rocks?"

Eric hung his head

"And that Friday?"

When Eric went for his daily hook-up that warm November day, Petra told him that she wanted to throw an engagement party. She wanted him to meet all her friends and family.

While I was doing my Christmas shopping. What a Black Friday bargain I got.

"I realized she had to be crazy," he said. "I had only been seeing her for a few weeks. Who announces an engagement like that? I told her I loved my wife and I wouldn't leave her."

Right. He loved me so much that he just had to cheat on me.

"What about the resort in the Maritimes?"

"When Petra told me about it, I said there was no way I would go on vacation with her. We argued."

They fought. She slapped him. He pushed her. She fell backward, cracking her skull against the granite counter.

Eric hunched over, his arms wrapped around his middle as if he were trying to keep his guts from spilling out.

"It was an accident, I swear!"

You bastard.

In a panic, Eric picked up her dead body and stuffed her into the trunk of her car. He drove to the state forest and dumped the body. Then he drove back and put the car into the garage.

And that's when he took his shirt off, and not just because he was sweating. The shirt was covered in Petra Rooney's blood.

What he didn't know was that Petra, truly believing she had met the man of her dreams, had already ordered the cake. From me.

The hazards of having different last names.

An officer read Eric his rights and took him away in handcuffs. I leaned my head against the mirror trying to be as quiet as possible as I cried torrents.

Detective Rogers came through the door in the back of the observation room. He handed me a glass of water. I gulped it down.

"I think I might need something a bit stronger," I said.

Detective Rogers smiled, a glint in those fabulous green eyes. "Well, if you're willing to go outside, I know a nice little bistro around the corner."

~

The Friday after Thanksgiving is Black Friday.

ICED IN

BY RUTH M. MCCARTY

Libby Fisher pulled the curtains back, flinching at the blinding snow and crusted ice the April Fools' storm had dumped during the night. It had come without warning—at least to her. Maybe back home in Massachusetts the meteorologists were storm drunk by now, but here in Maine, where she had no cable, no internet, and no phone service, the storm had been an unwanted surprise.

She'd woken in the middle of the night to the machine gun tapping of hail and the penetrating cold of the cabin. The electricity had failed, and with it the space heater she'd brought from home.

She'd rolled toward Sam's side of the bed, hoping to snuggle up to his warmth, instead finding the cold empty space his death had left.

Libby shivered now, pulled off her nightgown and tugged on the jeans and sweater she'd been wearing the night before. The hail had turned to freezing rain, and was already coating the tree branches. She'd have to hurry out to the shed to bring in as much firewood as she could carry.

Once she got the wood-burning stove going, she'd make a cup of tea. Something to warm her while she waited for the cabin to warm. As if she could ever be warm again.

Libby had come to pack their personal belongings. To put the cabin up for sale.

Sam had been killed in a robbery gone wrong in the artsy town of Houghton where they owned an antique store.

"After drug money," the police had said. It had been weeks and they still hadn't found the intruders who had tied Sam up and shot him dead.

Shot him dead. The words rang in her head, a mantra now, whenever Libby thought about the robbery. Why did they have to kill him?

Sam's winter jacket and tan leather work boots were by the back door that faced the lake, left there from the last time they'd come. Her heart ached at the sight of the worn leather. She pulled on the boots and laced them tight. They were too big, but she hadn't brought winter boots with her this time. She'd worn sneakers. It was April 1st after all. She pulled on Sam's jacket, stopping to smell his scent, a combination of sawdust and pine. Tears fell, and she swiped them away. She had to get the wood and get back inside.

She found Sam's knitted cap in the right-hand pocket and put it on. She needed gloves, but couldn't think where they would be. God, she wished Sam was there. At least she knew the leather tarp to carry the firewood would be in the trunk Sam had built for the screened-in porch. It served as a coffee table, set between the two pressed-back antique wooden rockers they'd found in an abandoned storage unit they had bid on at an auction. They'd brought the rockers with them the last weekend they'd come.

Snow had sifted through the screens and onto the porch. Libby dusted it off the trunk and pulled out the tarp. Wrapped inside it were the suede leather gloves. "Thank you, Sam," she whispered.

With each step to the shed, the ice crackled as her feet broke through the thick ice blanketing the snow, and the freezing rain clung to her exposed face. She laid the tarp on the snow and yanked the firewood from its icy stack, thankful that the gloves protected her hands and that Sam had taught her how to bank a fire in the stove.

It took two trips to bring in enough firewood to last all day and hopefully through the night. After getting the fire started, she put the cast iron tea pot on the wood stove to boil. Then she filled two large pans with what water was left in the pipes, careful not to drain the whole thing and mess up the well.

She closed the door to the bedroom to keep the heat in the main room and after drinking her tea and eating a leftover stale doughnut, got down to the heartbreaking task she'd come to do—pack up their life.

She tackled the kitchen cabinets first. She'd be leaving most things—dishes, glasses, pots and pans, for the next owner. But the rare fish-shaped salt and pepper shakers they'd bought at a yard sale for pennies, would go home with her. "Perfect for a lake house," Sam had said. It broke her heart now. She rolled the shakers in the packing paper she'd brought then sat and cried. This was going to be harder than she thought—packing memories into a box.

By mid-morning, she'd gone through all the cabinets, leaving most things, before tackling the living room. She'd decorated it with overstuffed chairs and a small sofa bed loaded with pillows they'd bought in case they invited friends up over the summer. They'd bought the furniture for comfort and filled the walls with antique paintings and signs, and the shelves with collectibles and photos.

She picked up the picture of Sam fishing the day they signed the documents for the cabin. Sam looked so happy then. So full of life. She hugged the picture to her to chest.

She packed her books and collectibles, stacking the heavy boxes by the door until she was ready to go in the morning, weather permitting. She left the rowboat oars on the wall. Would leave the blue speckled enamel coffee pot. Packed the wooden basket with the stuff from the small desk that doubled as an extra table they'd brought on their last trip. It had been in the storage unit with the rockers.

Libby's stomach growled. She looked out the window, and saw the clouds were finally lightening and light fluffy snow was falling on top of the ice. The storm would be over soon, but not soon enough to leave today. At first light in the morning she'd be up and finish whatever packing she'd have left to do.

She knew it could take days, maybe even weeks, before the electricity came back on, so she got her kerosene lamps ready for the night. The long stick matches were on a shelf in the kitchen, and candles, if needed, were in the catch-all closet she hadn't gotten to yet.

Libby ate a peanut butter and jelly sandwich for lunch, even though she had no appetite. She drank a glass of the milk before taping up cardboard boxes to start packing the closet. She'd leave the linens. The new owners would be happy and she really hadn't spent that much money on them. She'd leave the bars of soap, the jumbo size package of toilet paper and the first aid kit.

She really was leaving more behind than she was taking. It felt like she was leaving Sam behind. She grabbed the extra candles from the top shelf and put them on the kitchen table with the kerosene lamps. She would leave all of them here. One last check of the closet, then she could close the door on it. She reached into the corners, checking for lost items, and found a box of bullets.

She'd forgotten about them—and the gun. The loaded gun that Sam had hidden in the bedroom, loosely taped to the back of the headboard. She didn't want them. Wouldn't keep them. Didn't like it when Sam had shown her how to load the gun and how to slowly squeeze the trigger, and didn't like that he made her target shoot, even though she hated it. She got the gun and put it and the bullets in with her knitting, tucking them under her yarn. She'd drive to the local police station on her way out and turn them in, along with Sam's license to carry.

She made another cup of tea and sank into her chair. All that was left to pack was the bedroom. She'd purposely put it off. Packing her clothes would be easy, Sam's not so much. Just opening the closet door brought his scent into the room. She guessed she'd sleep on the sofa tonight, covered in the blankets they had shared so many nights, keeping warm by the wood stove, all the while wishing she could be keeping warm in the bedroom with Sam.

SHE REACHED for his old sweater and put it on, breathing in Sam's lingering cologne. If she closed her eyes, she could imagine him being there.

Something rattled in the pocket. She reached in and ran her fingers through the items. Smooth yet sharp. Took out a handful. Nearly fell over when she realized what they were.

The diamonds.

Sam had hidden the diamonds from the storage unit in his ratty old sweater. She thought the men who killed Sam had taken them the night they killed Sam.

Her eyes filled with tears. Sam knew she'd find them if anything happened to him.

They had been the high bidder on the unit. Had no idea what was inside. Lawfully, everything belonged to them now, but when she'd opened the strongbox and saw the diamonds, she wanted to bring them right to the police station. Sam had talked her out of it. "Wait," he'd said. "Let me investigate who they belong to."

Tears welled. "Oh, Sam, I wish we turned them in," she said aloud.

Libby worked the rest of the afternoon. After ignoring her growling stomach for hours she opened a can of beans with the hand can opener, then opened both ends of a can of brown bread with raisins. A childhood staple at her house. Of course, her mother had added cut up hotdogs to the beans. She and Sam had laughed about romantic candlelit dinners when they'd purchased bags of canned goods for the cabin. She threw a couple more logs into the stove and poked them around, making sure the fire was good and hot. Then she grabbed the black cast iron frying pan and sliced the brown bread to fry until crispy, before adding the beans to heat.

After eating, she poured a glass of wine from the bottle she'd opened the night before. She sat on the couch, lit one of the kerosene lanterns, put her heavy black flashlight on the table for when she needed to use the bathroom, took a sip of her wine, then picked up her knitting, hoping she could see in the dim light.

Libby's head snapped toward the window at the sound of ice crunching and the low hum of a vehicle approaching. She saw headlights turning into her driveway. It had to be the sheriff's department checking on the few people who lived scattered around the lake.

Who else would be out on a night like this?

Jumpy since Sam's death, and the stress of being alone, she wasn't taking any chances. She pulled the cold metal gun from her knitting basket, then put it in the empty sweater pocket. A calmness came over her as she ran her fingers through the diamonds in her other pocket, gulped some more wine and waited for the knock on the door.

When it came, she still jumped. "Who's there?" she yelled.

"Mrs. Fisher?" A man's voice came through the door. "It's the sheriff. My deputy and I are checking on all the cabins tonight. Crazy storm and all."

"I'm all set," Libby answered. "Leaving in the morning."

"Just need to see you, then we'll be on our way."

There was no way she was opening the door. Libby got up, ready to peek through the window, when the door crashed open and two men rushed in.

"Start searching," the short stocky one said.

The tall one pushed past her and opened the linen closet door, whipping sheets, towels and blankets to the floor. Trashing everything. He then headed into the bedroom and Libby heard the scraping of drawers being pulled from the bureau.

"Where's the diamonds?" The shorter one with a twisted nose yelled at her.

"Diamonds? I don't what you're talking about," she lied, hoping to sound convincing.

The man slapped her face so hard she banged to the floor. He yanked her up, shaking her shoulders. "The strong box. Where it is? And don't say it's back at your house because we looked. It's not there."

Libby felt like she couldn't breathe. Her house. They'd been to her house. "Who are you? What do you want?"

"We want the strong box from the storage unit."

"The storage unit?" She played dumb.

"Yes. Don't be stupid like your husband," he said, and let her go. "We know you bought the unit at auction. Give us the diamonds, then we'll leave you alone."

Her heart stopped. They had killed Sam and would kill her, too. She had to think fast.

Libby heard glass shatter in the other room, and the man in front of her turned to look. She grabbed the heavy flashlight and clobbered him with all her strength as he turned back. His knees buckled and he fell to the floor with a crash.

The other man came running. Libby reached into her pocket and pulled out the gun. He stopped. Looked wary.

She pointed the gun at him. "I'll use this if I have to."

She could tell from his dead eyes that he was waiting for the right moment to snatch the gun from her.

"Give us the strongbox," he said, in a soothing tone. "Then we'll leave and you'll never see us again."

The man took a step forward. "That gun's gonna get heavy pretty fast," he said, looking at her outstretched arm.

She licked her dry lips and said, "Well, I'll have to use it then."

They wouldn't be letting her go. They'd killed Sam, and trashed her house and the shop. They would kill her the minute she handed over the strong box.

"What the hell is in it that's worth killing over?" she asked.

He sneered, stepping closer to Libby. "You know what's in it. The diamonds."

Sweat dripped down her arms. She wouldn't get out alive—she knew too much. "I don't know anything about any diamonds. The strongbox must be out in the shed," she lied. "There's a bunch of boxes we haven't gone through yet."

His eyes gleamed. He lunged toward her. She held her breath and pulled the trigger. The other man struggled as he stood. She shot him too. Still holding the gun, her heart beating right out of her chest, she checked each man for a pulse. Sam had taught her well.

Libby grabbed her keys and bag and headed through the snow to her car. She looked back at the house and made a decision. Sam wanted her to have the diamonds and he'd died for them. She wouldn't turn them over to the police. She'd keep them, like Sam wanted her to. Everyone who know about them was dead.

She reached into her sweater pocket, and then threw them onto the fresh powdered snow before jumping in her four-wheel drive van.

She drove into town, praying the vehicle wouldn't go off the road. She told the officer on duty what had happened and he sent two SUV's patrols out to the lake. Her hands shook as she took the coffee the officer handed her. She went over her story again, and had him call the police in Houghton to let them know she knew who had killed Sam.

Libby stayed in town that night and the next. Got a ride back to the lake the morning after the police had finished working the crime scene and the cleaners she'd hired had removed all traces of the horrible night.

The men she had shot were known criminals and Libby was thankful the police believed she shot them in self-defense. There wouldn't be any charges against her.

Over the past two nights, she'd made a few decisions. She was going to keep the cabin.

She'd lease a building in town to open an antique store to

see if she could make a go of it. It had been her and Sam's plan for the future, she'd just be doing it a lot earlier and alone.

She looked up. The sun felt good on her face. Soon she'd be able to find the diamonds in the melted snow. She stepped inside the cabin and started putting her life back together.

April Fools' Day falls on April 1st.

THE MOST WONDERFUL CRIME OF THE YEAR

BY SHARON DAYNARD

Saturday, December 18

"Christmas." Nick Caedwalla spat out the word like it was cheap whiskey as he took in the 360-degree view from the rooftop conservatory of his Winter Street Towers penthouse.

On a clear day or moonlit night, there wasn't an inch of Wintertide that escaped the 39-year-old crime kingpin's scrutiny. What little got passed him, toadies and bootlickers shared to curry favors. He chronicled all of it, the bad and the good, for purposes of blackmail, extortion and payback.

He slipped a pair of white cotton gloves over the nitrile exam gloves he wore, shoved a black money pouch into the jacket pocket of his Santa suit, tucked his prematurely white shoulder-length hair under his stocking cap and a Glock 21SF in the concealed waistband holster at small of his back. Against his better judgement as a connoisseur of rare bourbons and aged whiskeys, he emptied a nip of Firestarter into his mouth, swished the cheap cinnamon booze, gargled and swallowed it hard. Between the chintzy red flannel outfit, the matted, faux white beard and the chosen libation of underage drinkers and douchebags everywhere burning a hole in his gut, he was amazed his body hadn't spontaneously combusted in revulsion.

He put on a dime store pair of matte-finish, black sunglasses, stepped into the penthouse's private elevator and rode it to the underground garage singing "Santa Claus is Coming to Town" in a tone so menacing the neck hairs on anyone within earshot would have stood on end.

A quick jaunt up the garage's pedestrian walkway would have brought him onto Winter Street, from there it was a short walk downtown. Any other day, quick and direct would have been his chosen route. But today quick and direct brought the possibility of encountering any one of the Tower's overzealous residents who were 911-happy when it came to trespassers. It also brought the prospect of someone at street level recalling, hours or even days later, a bargain-basement Santa exiting the parking garage of one of the city's priciest properties.

Opting for the less-than-scenic route downtown, Caedwalla skulked through shadows as he made his way to the Exit Only door at the rear of the garage. The handful of minutes the detour cost him was far outweighed by the gold-ring opportunity of being spared even one offkey caroler, in-your-face push-cart huckster or roaming horde of day-trippers.

A tattletale-wail echoed through the garage as he pushed the metal door open and checked the Eisenhower dollar coin he'd duct-taped four hours earlier across the strike plate to keep it from locking. Shrill and sharp, the door bid him good riddance as he stepped outside onto a ribbon of freshly-plowed pavement that stretched behind five adjacent buildings and ended in a service alley dotted with dumpsters ripe with refuse and rodents. That alley opened onto Winter Street. No one would give two shakes of a rat's ass if they saw a soused Santa staggering out of an alley after taking a leak.

As it was, the only person Caedwalla encountered in the service alley was a Santa slumped over the steering wheel of a rusted-out pickup that looked like it was held together with duct tape and Bondo. Between the scrap tires, empties, cigarettes butts and long-dead leaves littering its bed, the truck might have served as a makeshift dumpster. The battered cooler, heavy-duty chains and Louisville Slugger snugged between the cab and driver's side wheel tub were worth more than the truck. It was hard to tell if the guy inside were sleeping one off or dead. Not that Caedwalla cared.

Like ants on a discarded half-eaten candy cane, locals and out-of-towners were swarming downtown for Winterfest—a season's worth Christmas frivolity crammed into one miserable weekend. Adding to the madness were hundreds of Santas in every shape, size and state of inebriation dressed in full regalia for the annual Christmas Pub Crawl. He hadn't made it fifty feet down the crowded street when some idiot clanked a bell in his ear and wished him good cheer before nodding down at a red kettle, as if the only thing standing between a merry Christmas and Ebenezer Scrooge repossessing the holiday was his spare change

Caedwalla shrugged a whatever and pulled a Firestarter nip from his pocket. In a spectacular display of alcohol-fueled jackassery, he repeatedly tried to cram the small plastic bottle through the narrow slit in the kettle's lid. He gave up after more than a few bystanders captured his one-man show on their cell phones, knowing it was only a matter of time before the vaudeville-like act blew up on social media.

With the sincerest of slurred apologies, Caedwalla opened the nip and toasted the crowd with "To humbug and horseshit," before losing his balance and spilling most of the whiskey down his faux white beard. What little was left, he swallowed and let out a "Hot damn!" as he ambled down Winter Street.

Like a politician trailing in the polls on election day, he reached out and shook the hand of everyone he stumbled into, making sure they got a generous whiff of cinnamon booze as he indulged in the lost art of misdirection. It was still so damn easy. Even covered with two pairs of gloves, his fingertips were still as quick and nimble as when he was sixteen and working a bump and lift on subway cars. He could have gone on for hours moving from one hapless mark to the next for the sheer sport of it. Instead, he stopped outside the Wintertide Savings and Loan and surveyed his reflection in the bank's glass door. He looked pretty much like every other idiot downtown sporting cheap black sunglasses and dressed as the patron saint of binge eating and empty threats. Granted, his outfit was missing Santa's big black belt, but you got what you paid for when you shopped at a discount store.

He plucked a toothpick from his left pocket, dangled it from the corner of his mouth and sauntered through the bank's lobby with the three-sheets-to-the-wind swagger of a well-lubed lush.

"Merry Christmas, ya filthy animals," he garbled his holiday greeting.

Each of the three tellers looked from him to the clock on the wall and heaved audible sighs of revulsion before refocusing their attention on the customers in front of them.

"Like it's my fault the bank closes at noon on Saturdays," Caedwalla groused, stumbling through a maze of velour-roped stanchions to the end of the line. Swaying on his feet in an ever-increasing circle, he watched a banker cross the floor and lock the front door.

"Stop your jabbering and keep the line moving," Caedwalla hollered at the tellers.

The hag in front of Caedwalla turned around, surveyed him from his pom-pommed red stocking cap to the bright yellow laces of his black leather Doc Martens and gave a priggish roll of her beady eyes. He, in turn, gave her a fish-eyed once-over.

"If you haul ass, sister, you can probably snag the last Santa suit at Setzer's in a size extra-bitchy."

She huffed, turned her back to him and raised her pointy chin in the air.

He responded with a crude gesture that drew a gasp from a mother with two kids in tow.

Wanting nothing more at that moment than to dig as deep as he could under the old bat's liver-spotted skin, he belched long and hard and belted out the "Twelve Days of Christmas" without regard to the order of days or their appointed gifts, as he surveyed the bank.

Potted poinsettias littered desktops, counters and teller stations. Garlands of greeting cards wrapped around columns, doorframes and windows. In the corner, a sap-dripping 10-foot Balsam Fir covered in vintage mercury glass ornaments and seizure-inducing blinking white lights just begged to be knocked over.

On the wall next to a fire alarm, a tarnished brass plaque stated the Wintertide Savings and Loan was the oldest operating bank in the city, having been founded in 1885. From the looks of the place the alarm system and corroded pendent sprinklers hadn't been updated since its grand opening.

"I ain't got all day," he griped. "If I miss Christmas Trivia at the Crawl, you're all getting coal in your socks."

Of the three tellers, two were in their early twenties, the third was somewhere between fifty and a hundred. Considering Winterfest was the equivalent of Small Business Saturday for Wintertide merchants, he could guarantee both Kelsie's and Aubrey's working drawers were crammed with everything from ones to one-hundred-dollar bills and their bottom drawers were unlocked and stuffed with cash. Neither would think twice about handing over all of it to him. He doubted either possessed the temerity to slip in a dye pack, even if it meant a bonus in their next paycheck. Kelsie and Aubrey were a bank robber's wet dream.

Margaret, on the other hand, was a nightmare wrapped in a red and green plaid muumuu. He was willing to bet everything he owned that Margaret toed the company line. If there was more than a grand in her working drawer, it'd be the first time in her lackluster career. And not only was her bottom drawer locked, the key was probably tucked in her bra, where no man dared go.

Margaret didn't smile when he toddled up to her station. She didn't offer a cordial hello or ask what she could do for him. She set her jaw, flared her nostrils and glowered. She cocked her head left, right and back to center as if squaring off with him before hissing, "Yes?"

Had Margaret been a tad friendlier, a tad more of a Peggy, a Maggie or a Molly, things would have gone so much smoother. He would have conducted his business and been on his way without incident. Instead, he stood there rotating the toothpick in his mouth, staring her down through Blues Brothers shades.

"And a friggin' holly jolly to you too, Margaret." The toothpick took a slow ride to the corner of his mouth before he asked, "Got any free samples?"

Margaret's face twisted into a knot as if it were the hundredth time that morning she'd heard the same corny line. Still, she could've played along. She could've offered him a lighthearted shrug, an impish scrunch of her needle-sharp nose or even a goddam promotional pen. Instead, she hoisted the right half of her unibrow.

"Tell you what, Chewbacca." He paused, as if deep in contemplation, and chomped on the toothpick. "You do exactly as Santa says and there'll be a weed whacker under your Christmas tree for that forestache."

He leaned in closer and planted the money pouch on the counter. "You're gonna fill this with cash. And you're gonna smile the whole time. Hell, you're gonna to chuckle 'cause if you don't…" He pulled the Glock from the small of his back and tapped the muzzle on the countertop. "I don't give two squirts about it being the holidays, I'll blow your friggin' head off. Understand?"

Margaret nodded.

Caedwalla lurched forward with a throaty dry heave that promised so much more, ensuring Kelsie and Aubrey looked anywhere but his direction and affording himself a bird's-eye view of Margaret's working drawer. He watched in mild amusement as she tore open the zippered pouch and crammed the loose one-dollar bills inside, then their banded counterparts before moving on to the fives, tens and twenties. And just like he'd figured, there wasn't a hundred or a fifty in her drawer. But there was a lone thousand-dollar strap of tens. He pretended not to notice the grin tugging at the corners of her carp mouth as she ever so gently slipped it inside the pouch. Or that she held her breath when she zipped the pouch closed and slid it across the counter to him.

For shits and giggles he thought about telling her to open the bottom drawer, but what was the point? He'd gotten what he came for.

"Was that so hard, Margaret?"

She shook her head and smiled a smile so broad and gloating it took every ounce of restraint he had not to toss the strap of tens back at her and tell her to screw herself.

"One more thing, Margaret. If you even think about pulling an alarm before I'm in the next county, it'll be New Year's before they finish scraping your shit for brains off the walls. Like I said, I don't give two squirts."

He snugged the Glock back into its holster, grabbed the pouch and strolled slow and cool to the front door. With a magician's sleight of hand, he dropped the toothpick into his left pocket and plucked a gnawed one from his right as he wheeled around to get one last look at that smug smile on Margaret's face.

With a smirk that dwarfed hers, he flicked the toothpick in the air, drew the Glock and fired a deadeye shot.

~

Sirens whimpered off in the distance as Caedwalla backtracked his way up Winter Street, maneuvering through the crowd, when he heard the cap-gun pop of the dye pack concealed in the hollowed-out strap of tens go off in the pouch.

Wisps of red smoke trailed him as he turned into the service alley. Not that anyone noticed. They were too busy cheering on and gushing over two of the Wintertide Aquarium's far from remarkable penguins dressed as elves, roller skating down Winter Street at a slower than snail's pace. Refusing to budge, the prima-donnas stood steadfast and aloof, ignoring the limp fish their handlers dangled as an incentive to keep moving. Caedwalla couldn't have asked for better timing, the longer the two loitered, the longer the crowd stayed put and distracted, allowing him to go about his business unnoticed.

He opened the driver's door of the pickup, jerked the unconscious guy's head from the steering wheel and spoke into in his ear. "Yes, Virginia, there is a Santa Claus. He's doing ten-to-fifteen for armed bank robbery."

The guy never even stirred when Caedwalla plunged a syringe of naloxone deep into his thigh to counteract the elephant tranquilizer that sedated him hours ago. It'd be a good ten minutes before the jolly bastard came to. Plenty of time to make certain Sleepy Santa himself, let alone a jury, would be hard put to believe he hadn't robbed the bank.

Caedwalla filled the guy's jacket pockets with the wallets, watches and cell phones he'd lifted on his way to the bank. Not that Sleepy Santa deserved the credit for the impressive haul, but Christmas being only a week away had Caedwalla feeling generous. He unzipped the pouch, dropped it on the guy's lap and closed the pickup's door. A grin cut across his face as the truck's cab filled with red smoke and the pungent odor of spent firecrackers. A GPS tracker instead of a dye pack would have been so much savvier, but nowhere near as much fun.

Caedwalla waited until he'd figured Sleepy Santa had breathed in enough of the stuff to have been rendered unconscious from smoke inhalation under normal circumstances, before he opened the door for some fresh air. Red dye bled deep into Caedwalla's white gloves as he grabbed fistfuls of stained and charred bills from the pouch and tossed them into the alley for the wind to find.

Making damn sure red dye transferred from his gloves to every surface of the truck he touched, Caedwalla gripped the steering wheel, grabbed the half-empty bottle of Firestarter wedged between the dashboard and the windshield and drizzled more than a little on the guy's fake white beard before shoving the open bottle back where he'd found it. He pulled down the visor, replaced the set of keys tucked in it with the Glock, tossed the keys down by the gas pedal along with the guy's sunglasses, and slid open the rear window.

Mindful to retain as much gunshot residue a possible on his once-white gloves, Caedwalla exercised great care peeling them from the exam gloves on his hands and sliding them on the guy's naked hands. Cautious and calculated, he pinched each of the guy's newly-gloved fingertips and pressed down on both the palms and backs his hands.

Caedwalla stripped down to jeans and a hideous Christmas sweater—perfect for blending in with the rest of the yahoos in town for Winterfest. He buried the miserable costume beneath a few rank bags of trash in the dumpster and pulled a burner phone from his pocket. Before destroying the SIM card, he placed an anonymous muffled call to 911, reporting what looked like red smoke coming from a pickup in an alley off Winter Street.

He'd done his good deed for the day.

Strutting down the service alley and back along the ribbon of pavement, Caedwalla swore he could still hear Margaret screeching under a geyser of frigid water from the sprinkler head he'd shot off.

One week earlier
Saturday, December 11

An Alvin and the Chipmunks, nails-on-chalkboard, rendition of "Jingle Bell Rock" blared over speakers as Nick Caedwalla sat upright and rigid on an ornate throne. Jaw clenched, brow furrowed and hands balled into tight fists on the armrests, he swore he was seated centerstage in the deepest, darkest pit of hell that existed for psychopaths who'd put up Christmas trees before their Thanksgiving turkeys were dressed and in the oven, deviants who'd included mind-numbing, multipage family newsletters in their Christmas cards, and the legions of deplorable department store and shopping mall Santas who'd systematically indoctrinated generations of children into the Cult of Claus.

"Welcome to hell, gentlemen," he grouched to the pair of toughs standing sentry on either side of him at the Wintertide Music Hall. Despite the whimsical reindeer antler headbands the two wore, they looked like they were on work release from the North Pole Penitentiary. "Rudolph" was scribbled in thick black marker across one thug's nametag and "Rudolph's Pal" across the other's.

"Come the twenty-sixth, the Winter Street Benevolent Society is out of the business of Christmas. Let some other sap waste their time and money on this, this…" Caedwalla's arms swept wide encompassing all of the hall. "This tripe."

Freeloaders, layabouts and slackers, along with their assorted offspring and wards filled every seat. Holy terrors in campy holiday outfits raced up and down the aisles, draped themselves over balcony railings and threw epic meltdowns while they waited like rabid ferrets to unload their list of Christmas demands on him.

The Winter Street Benevolent Society should've been the crown jewel in Nick Caedwalla's crime empire, instead it'd become the bane of his existence. Laundering money under the guise of a Christmas charity worked like a charm until it flipped on him.

That first year he received a few sappy, chicken-scratched letters in the mail. In return, he hand-delivered token gifts to the paupers on Christmas morning, dressed in a jovial, hand-tailored, burgundy sharkskin suit. He made sure media outlets covered it. The second, he begrudgingly sprang for a holiday party in the common room at the Towers, complete with a rented Santa, gingerbread cookies and gift bags. Despite the logistical nightmare, he managed to personally deliver a gift to each of the fifty-three leeches on his list while playing up his Saint Nick schtick for the cameras.

The third year it snowballed. Letters from deadbeats, derelicts and down-and-outers of every age and station found their way to him, begging for his generosity and kindness. Caedwalla needed a function hall to accommodate the number of losers who wrote to him. The only way he got a gift to each and every parasite on Christmas morning was to enlist his cronies to help with deliveries. But he made damn sure it was Saint Nick, and not his elves, that made the news.

It was that third misbegotten year that got the WSBS audited. Unlike the barflies who marveled at his IQ of 198 and photographic memory, the IRS auditors weren't impressed when he told them he kept the financial records in his head. And despite being able to recall every detail of every WSBS check he'd written, every deposit and deduction taken, along with the name and address of every moocher he'd ever coughed up a gift for, they raked him over the coals like he was Al Capone.

This year, the WSBS needed the Wintertide Music Hall for the afternoon. Granted, it took a bit of creative persuasion in the form of a road trip to an abandoned quarry while hogtied and hooded in the trunk of a car, but not only did the musical hall's owner cancel two sold-out matinee performances of the Nutcracker, he also saw his way to provide the hall free of charge. He even offered dozens of actors to dress as elves, snowmen and reindeer to entertain the families, and a professional photographer to take complimentary pictures of the little ones on Santa's lap. Hell, he was even willing to play the part of Santa. And all of it pro bono if it set things right with Nick Caedwalla. After making it clear things were far from right, Caedwalla took him up on everything, but playing the part of Santa. This year, Christmas was going to be on his terms.

"Silence!" Caedwalla's voice carried like thunder over the din, reverberating through the music hall. He drummed his fingers on the throne's armrests, waiting for compliance. It was time to get the charade over with. He let out a low, guttural growl of contempt. "If you brought a Christmas list hold it up." His jaw shifted left and right as sheet after sheet of paper sprung up. "Hand it to your adult for fulfillment." A venomous smirk tore across his face as he took in the puzzled faces.

"When your row is called, you and your adult will proceed in an orderly fashion to the center aisle. You will remain composed and quiet until summoned onto the stage, at which time your adult will legibly print your name and address in my guest book for benefit of the IRS. I, of course, know who you are, what you've done and where you sleep."

He paused, giving the revelation time to sink into their feeble brains.

"Upon being placed on my lap by your adult, you will make one gift request. I repeat, one. You will smile for the camera, retrieve your commemorative photograph and vacate the premises. Anyone who whines, stomps their feet or prattles on with their gift list can kiss Christmas goodbye. Have I made myself clear?" Based on the dropped jaws and pitiful crying, he had. "And no more leaving out milk and cookies on Christmas Eve. Saint Nick likes bourbon. Neat."

~

After what seemed like an eternity, Caedwalla checked his watch, realized he was barely two hours into the freakshow and let loose a barrage of obscenities that caused even the Rudolphs to blush. He could have saved himself a mountain of aggravation if he'd announced at the start that he already knew what they were getting for Christmas–Disappointment with a capital D.

He'd had it with kids who burst into tears, crumpled in a heap on the floor or bolted off stage and those who shrugged, looked desperately to their adult for rescue or uttered the first mindless gift that popped into their vapid little heads.

"Hey, F-bomb," the photographer called out to him. "How

about losing the resting Grinch face? A smile never killed anyone. Just say cheese."

"Cheeeeeesssssse." The word slithered off Caedwalla's tongue at a funeral pace, contorting his mouth into a twisted grin that would have curled the devil's toes, as he contemplated what the photographer would miss more, index fingers or an eye.

His glare fixed on the photographer, Caedwalla waited until every last bit of color drained from the shutterbug's face before summoning the next charity case onto the stage. The kid looked about six and on the thin side, coming nowhere close to filling out the holiday hand-me-downs he wore. His sister, babysitter or teen mom clutched the chest of her coat as if she was afraid it'd fall from her waif-like frame if she didn't. Concealer did little to mask the remnants of a mouse beneath her right eye.

The kid reached out, shook Caedwalla's hand and introduced himself as Chance Hollenbeck. Once placed on Caedwalla's lap, he pulled a folded sheet of paper from his pocket.

"I said no lists, kid. Doll, ball, book or boardgame. Pick one, smile for the camera and hit the road."

"I don't want a toy. I want my dog back."

Caedwalla looked from the kid to the young woman with a WTF raise of his brow.

"We talked about this, Chance," she prompted the kid. "You want a sled."

The kid shook his head. "I want my dog."

"Maybe the kid wants a dogsled," Rudolph's Pal quipped.

Caedwalla wasn't amused.

"His name is Bubbles and I want him back."

"Look, kid, I'm not in the poodle finding business."

"He's not a poodle. He's a fierce guard dog."

"Named Bubbles?" Rudolph snickered. "What's he guard, rubber duckies?" A glacial side-eye from Caedwalla shut him up.

"He's just a stray that followed us home from the park," the young woman said. "Chance was blowing bubbles and the dog chased them. We were only going to take Bubbles in for—"

"What happened to your dog?" Caedwalla asked the kid.

"Daryl took him."

Caedwalla looked again from the kid to the woman.

She offered him a jiggle of her head. "Daryl had nothing to do with it. Daryl's terrified of Bubbles," she whispered. "Bubbles never lets Chance out of his sight. He sleeps on Chance's bed, walks him to school and waits outside his classroom window no matter how bad the weather. Bubbles wasn't waiting for Chance when he got out of school a few weeks ago."

"Who's Daryl?"

"Mom's boyfriend," the kid mumbled.

"Ex-boyfriend," she corrected. "Tell Saint Nick you want a sled, Chance, so we can leave."

Before the kid could say anything, the next brat in line, a girl, stomped up onto the stage. "It's my turn!"

"It's not your turn until I say it is and I say you just lost yours." Caedwalla hooked a thumb, motioning both the girl, and the woman she was with, to leave.

"You can't tell me or my nanny what to do. My name is Savannah Sherwood and my daddy's the mayor. It's my turn. Now!"

"She's only seven," the nanny apologized. "She's just so excited. Aren't you, Savannah?"

"No!" The girl stomped her foot. "Nobody cares about your stupid dog." She stuck her tongue out at Chance and turned on Caedwalla. "Get me a new phone, a floor lounger, cosmic glitter bath bombs, a coding kit, a speed cube puzzle, unicorn string lights, a—"

"You know what you're getting?" Caedwalla cut her off. "Nothing."

"You can't do that. You're not the real Santa Claus."

Caedwalla's face scrunched in a far from playful grimace. "Wanna bet?"

"My daddy says you're a bad man. Mommy says you belong in jail."

"And now they're getting nothing for Christmas." Caedwalla rolled his eyes as Rudolph and Rudolph's Pal dragged Savannah Sherwood, kicking and screaming off stage, with her speechless nanny in close pursuit.

"Lesson to the rest of you. Don't test my patience!" Caedwalla warned the audience before looking back to the kid on his lap. "What kind of a dog is Bubbles?"

The kid unfolded the sheet of paper and handed it to Caedwalla. "The best kind."

Caedwalla studied the picture on the Lost Dog flyer of the kid with his arms wrapped around the neck of a Cane Corso that was a black as December nights were long. It was easily 150-pounds of brute muscle with mouth full of bone saw-sharp teeth. Between the dog's butchered ears and the scars on its muzzle and neck, it was apparent the dog had a brutal life before finding a home with the kid. "This monster is Bubbles?"

"He's not a monster!" the kid argued. "He's my friend."

Even the young woman objected. "Bubbles is the sweetest dog you can imagine."

Caedwalla looked back at the flyer finding her claim hard to believe. "That's one expensive dog. A top-quality Corsi with exceptional lineage can run as high as eighty-five hundred dollars in certain markets."

"Bubbles was a stray, not a show dog," the young woman said.

"Where's your dad, kid?"

The kid shrugged.

Caedwalla returned the gesture. "That's okay. I didn't have a dad. I had a revolving door of uncles. Most treated me like an afterthought, but a few went out of their way to backhand me every chance they got. Daryl ever hurt you?".

The kid shook his head. "Bubbles wouldn't let him. He bit Daryl because he hit my mom. That's why Daryl took him away."

The young woman shook her head again. "It was my fault. I shouldn't have laughed when Chance beat Daryl at checkers. He lashed out at me. Bubbles charged Daryl, knocked him down and latched onto his throat. It took close to ten minutes of coaxing for Bubbles to release him. Bubbles could have ripped Daryl's throat out, but didn't."

"Daryl peed his pants," the kid added.

"I bet he did. So, where's Daryl?"

"We haven't seen him since I threw him out that night two weeks ago."

"And Daryl's last name?"

Her lower lip trembled as if it were struggling to hold back an answer. It was the kid that offered him up. "Clark."

"Daryl Clark." Caedwalla stroked the impeccably groomed, 3-day silvery-white stubble on his chin, trying to place a face and a rap sheet with the name. "A greasy puke about my size with a shit-eating grin you want to beat off his face with a shovel very time you see him? A petty thief and all-around loser? Spends most of his paycheck at a dive called The Wingman?"

The young woman nodded.

"Is Daryl's on your naughty list?" the kid asked

"He is now." Caedwalla motioned for the photographer to snap a picture and lowered the kid off his lap. "No promises, but I'll see what I can do about finding your dog. How about you find the Rudolphs for me while your mom waits for your picture."

The kid nodded and pulled a toy compass from his pocket. "That girl's daddy is wrong. You're not a bad man. My mom says there aren't any bad people, just people who are lost. You can have my compass, Saint Nick. It always points to the North Pole so you can find your way home."

Caedwalla looked at the dollar store find the kid put in his hand as if it were fresh dog shit on the bottom of his shoe.

"If Bubbles gets hungry while you're delivering toys," the kid offered his parting advice, "he likes cheeseburgers with ketchup and pickles. No onions. They make him burp."

The young woman waited until her son was out of earshot to snap at Caedwalla. "Give me the compass."

"It's mine. The kid gave it to me."

"You're not lost, you're heartless. What am I supposed to tell Chance when he finds a sled under the tree instead of Bubbles?"

"I didn't promise the kid anything. I said I'd see what I could do. Ever think maybe his dog wouldn't be missing if you brought home a respectable man?"

"Since you're handing out false hope for the holidays, you know what I'd like for Christmas, Mr. Caedwalla? A respectable man from a good family that can see past a twenty-two-year-old with a six-year-old son."

Caedwalla gave a dismissive shake of his head.

"You think I haven't seen that look a thousand times while people mentally calculate how old I was when Chance was born. Let me save you the trouble, I was sixteen. Do you have any idea what it's like to find yourself pregnant after your first unchaperoned weekend at the lake with your friends? I didn't know the father's last name, let alone how to find him."

"Does it look like I care?"

"Did I mention my father's a minister in Indian Rock, Iowa? It's a picturesque little town of five thousand holier-than-thou busybodies."

"Blah, blah, blah."

"My parents decided the Christianly thing to do was to send me as far away as possible and arrange for the baby to be adopted into a loving family. I was onboard with everything right up until the nurse in the delivery room let me hold Chance. The next morning, I walked out of the hospital with my baby and never looked back. We moved from one homeless shelter to the next maxing out our stays until we ended up at the Third Street Shelter here in Wintertide."

"Boo-f'ing-hoo. I was orphaned at six, tossed from one foster care family to the next and living on the streets by the time I was thirteen."

"Every year I've sent my parents a Christmas card with picture of Chance and my phone number. They've never reached out to me or their grandson."

"You want my advice?" Caedwalla asked, looking past her at the endless line of brats. "Next time you tell that pathetic tale of woe try punching it up with a heaving sob here and there and breaking down at the end in crocodile tears. Maybe the next person will care, because I sure as hell don't."

"And you, Mr. Caedwalla, on Christmas morning when you're retelling your glorified, self-serving, rags-to-riches story for the cameras, try remembering what it was like when you had nothing and actually gave a damn. Maybe someone will revere you, because I sure as hell don't. Keep the compass," she said, walking away. "I imagine it's the only heartfelt gift you'll ever receive."

"Next!" Caedwalla's voiced boomed through the hall.

~

THE SOLES of Nick Caedwalla's boots peeled away like suction cups from the floor's waxy coating of spilled drinks and filth as he walked up to the bar and took a seat. He'd been generous when he called the Wingman a dive. Even after rummaging through the music hall's Lost and Found, he felt overdressed in the shabby jacket he wore over a tattered T-shirt. Slicked back with liquid hand soap and pulled into a man bun, his white hair looked a greasy, dishwater gray. There was enough dirt caked under his usually well-manicured nails, in the creases of his knuckles and ground into his jeans to fill the Grand Canyon, and he still looked like Mr. Clean in comparison to most of clientele.

He pulled a beat-up wallet from his back pocket and took a leisurely inventory of the bills inside. The bartender and anyone else silently counting along with him would've come up with a grand total $540. He dropped a fifty on the bar, returned the wallet to his pocket and ordered a shot of whiskey from the well.

He made it clear to the bartender he wasn't interested in talking sports and didn't give two shits about their wings. He was waiting for a ride. Eyes fixed straight ahead on the bar back mirror, he watched his back and waited for Daryl Clark. Two hours and six putrefied shots into his vigil, his gut had gone full circle from numb to burning and churning and back to numb. He'd checked his burner phone for a text at least a dozen times, getting a little more agitated each time.

He was about to grab his change off the bar and call it a night when someone bumped up hard against him, mumbled an apology and took the open stool next to him. Caedwalla ordered another whiskey and shot a sidelong glance at the gloating piece of shit that had just lifted his wallet with all the finesse of a fat-fingered gorilla with a bad case of the shakes.

"Firestarter on the rocks," the turd ordered, rotating a toothpick in his mouth.

Caedwalla rolled his eyes. Anyone else who'd poached a wallet that sloppy would have made a bee-line for the door and kept running until they were out of firing range. Either Daryl Clark was the ballsiest bastard in Wintertide or he actually thought he was that good at it. Caedwalla's money was on the latter.

A modicum of mirth lit his eyes as he imagined the pitiful look on Daryl Clark's face when he realized all he'd gotten was a couple of twenties and nine fifties even Helen Keller could have spotted as counterfeits, a long since expired driver's license and cancelled credit cards from the last wallet he'd lifted back in the day. The punch card for a free slice at Fat Tony's was a bonus. Years of being on the business end of a mugging taught Caedwalla to carry a decoy wallet. He also carried a 4-inch black ceramic-coated knife in an ankle sheath.

Daryl Clark was a piece of work all right, showing off the new pair of Doc Martens with bright yellow laces that magically found their way from a warehouse bin to his feet and crowing about his big plans to make a killing next weekend between being a shoo-in to win the Christmas Trivia contest at the Crawl and working the crowds in town for Winterfest. By working, it was obvious he meant pickpocketing.

Daryl Clark had it all figured out. He'd scouted out an alley without security cameras off Winter Street between the flower shop and the bookstore where he could park his pickup, flanked and concealed by a pair of dumpsters to keep it from being towed. Not only would it save him twenty dollars on parking at a garage, it'd give him a secluded place to get a few hours of shuteye after coming off the graveyard shift and still have plenty of time to check in at the Crawl, enjoy a complimentary breakfast buffet and an eyeopener before the trivia contest started around noon. He'd even managed to get ten dollars knocked off the already discounted price of a cheapo Santa suit and black sunglasses at Setzer's by ditching the black vinyl belt on the way to the registers.

"And," Daryl Clark droned on to the bartender, "everyone who finishes the Crawl gets a free t-shirt. That's one less gift I've gotta buy my mother." He tapped his index finger to his head.

The bartender didn't look impressed, neither did anyone else at the bar who'd been subjected to his upcoming itinerary.

"Ask me a question, any question about Christmas, and I bet I get it right," Daryl challenged anyone within earshot. "Movies, songs, anything." With no questions forthcoming, he asked and answered his own, marveling at his ability to answer each one correctly.

Caedwalla listened to the one-sided Q&A trying to figure out how an idiot like Daryl Clark managed to make off with a dog that wanted to shred him like a chew toy. Short of shooting the dog dead, there was only one plausible scenario and the thought of it turned his gut. As to why Daryl Clark would even want the dog, that was easy. The guy was stupid, but not a fool. A dog didn't get scars like the ones Bubbles had roughhousing with the other pups in the park. Bubbles had been bred, conditioned and trained for dog fighting. And a dog didn't live as long as Bubbles without being a championship contender. In the hands of the wrong kind of person, Bubbles was worth a fortune.

"How many ghosts is Ebenezer Scrooge visited by on Christmas Eve?" Caedwalla asked.

Daryl Clark snorted as if stunned by the simplicity of the question. "The ghosts of Past, Present and Future." He paused and with a smarmy smirk added, "And Jacob Marley. That makes four." He followed his answer with another snort.

Caedwalla made an annoying buzzer sound. "Wrong. One. The ghost of Jacob Marley. The other three were spirits."

Daryl Clark looked from Caedwalla to the bartender as if seeking confirmation or reversal on the call. The bartender shrugged which as far as Caedwalla was concerned was as good as winning the decision. Daryl Clark, on the other hand, dismissed the verdict, throwing his toothpick down on the bar next to Caedwalla. "*Like I give two squirts* about a rigged question. Spirits, ghosts, specters, they're all the same, pal."

It was Caedwalla's turn to shrug. He looked straight ahead at Daryl Clark's reflection in the mirror and held a wink long enough for it not be taken as anything other than a screw-you. "Whatever you say, chief."

Figuring he had a good ten to fifteen minutes before Daryl Clark came up a lame comeback, he ordered another shot and watched the guy stew. At least it put an end to the barside quiz show.

"Any chance theres's another pair of those boots in your truck?" the bartender asked, looking over the bar at Daryl's feet.

Daryl Clark shook his head and must've decided to move on from that snappy retort that wasn't materializing to making a few dollars. "I got something better than boots." He looked around the bar to see if anyone other than the bartender was in on the conversation and added, "Interested in money safe bag?"

Before the bartender could answer, Daryl Clark pulled what looked like an oversized, heavy-duty black canvas pencil bag from his jacket pocket and started shilling its virtues. "This here's a bulletproof, fireproof, waterproof and one-hundred percent indestructible space-age material that puts Kevlar to shame. And yours for a low fifty bucks."

Caedwalla rolled his eyes. What it was, was a money pouch made with a silicone-coated fiberglass material that was fire and water resistant. There was nothing bullet-proof or space-age about it. It sold for $15 at office supply stores.

"These ain't gonna last." Daryl Clark added a bit of pressure for that holiday impulse buy. The bartender passed even after the price was dramatically lowered to the point where Daryl Clark claimed he was losing money on the deal. "If you change your mind, you know where to find me."

Clark tossed the money pouch down on the bar and stuck a fresh toothpick in his mouth.

"You still got that dog?" the bartender asked. "I saved a few meat bones if you want them."

Daryl Clark shook his head. "That dog's been on a strict starvation diet. That brat Chance almost ruined that dog with all that fussing over him. Turned a born killer into a creampuff. But I beat the mean back into him."

"A dog's gotta eat," the bartender argued. "Is he out back in the truck? It's freezing out there."

"I don't give two squirts how cold it is. That dog ain't going anywhere warm until he starts making me money. When I leave here, I'm entering him in a fight. If he wins, he eats. If he loses, I sell him for pit bait. Either way I walk away with cash."

Caedwalla's hands balled into tight fists, ready to beat Daryl Clark until all that remained of him was another stain on the floor. Instead, he checked his phone and announced to the bartender that his friggin' ride was five blocks away. "How fast can you grill a cheeseburger to go?"

"Ten minutes. Five if it barely kisses the grill before I flip it."

"Two minutes," Caedwalla offered up the challenge. "I like my burgers rare with ketchup and pickles. No onions."

Caedwalla nodded his thanks when the bartender emerged from the kitchen and took a ten-dollar bill from Caedwalla's change on the bar. "Two minutes flat and blood rare," he announced, handing Caedwalla a Styrofoam box.

Caedwalla put the box down on the bar top, stuffed what was left of his fifty dollars in the front pocket of his jeans and reached in front of Daryl Clark for a napkin. "Have a good one." He nodded his goodbye, grabbed the box and walked out the door.

As he stepped outside, he could hear Daryl Clark hooting and howling. He wondered how long it would take before the jerk realized both the money pouch and his wallet were missing or that his gnawed toothpick had vanished.

It was easy enough to spot the Daryl Clark's pickup behind the bar. It was the only one with a Cane Corso chained to a U-bolt anchored to the truck's bed. The dog unleashed a visceral growl as Caedwalla approached.

"It's okay, Bubbles." He reached in his pocket and held out the plastic compass. "The kid sent me." Slow and deliberate, he inched the open take-out box toward the dog and waited as he finished off the burger in two desperate bites. "First thing I'm going to do is pop the lock on your collar. Then I'm going to get you to a vet I know. You don't want the kid seeing you like this. And then I'm going to take care of Daryl Clark."

A paperclip made easy work of the lock. He almost wished Daryl Clark would realize he'd been duped and charged out of the bar looking for him—he would've received such pleasure watching Bubbles tearing the dirtbag limb from limb. But in the absence of Daryl, the best he could do was take the knife from his ankle sheath and stick the driver's side front tire and tuck the kid's Lost Dog flyer with the word FOUND scrawled across it under a wiper blade.

~

Saturday, December 25

Nick Caedwalla pulled up into the projects in a black Escalade. Rudolph had the honors of being his driver that morning while he delivered gifts to one underserving brat after the other. He waited until the cameras and news crews left before he set out on his last stop.

He told Rudolph to blow the horn and if the kid didn't come out in two minutes, they were leaving. Chance Hollenbeck bolted out the front door of the building before Rudolph could comply with the order. Caedwalla looked through his black tinted window and shook his head. The kid was barefoot, still in his pajamas, waving his arms and grinning from ear to ear. He reminded Caedwalla a lot of what he was like before his mother OD'd thirty-three years ago to the day.

"I knew you'd find Bubbles!" the kid called out to him. "I knew you would."

Caedwalla waited until Rudolph opened his door to exit the SUV.

The kid's mother was maybe five steps behind, calling for him to put on the sneakers she had in her hands before he caught pneumonia. The kid didn't listen. He kept waving his arms and grinning as though Caedwalla showing up was the best thing that had ever happened to him.

"Sneakers," the kid's mother shouted. "Now!"

Caedwalla nodded in the direction of the young woman. "You heard her," he told the kid and watched him slide his feet into the oversized sneakers. Caedwalla imagined they probably fit better with a few pairs of thick winter socks. Or if the toes of the sneakers were stuffed with newspaper like he had to when he was on the streets.

The kid's mother stood there, not saying anything. She didn't have to, the why-are-you-even-here look on her face said it all.

Sneakers on, the kid raced up to Caedwalla, darting from

left to right, looking for Bubbles. The kid's chin quivered when he realized his dog wasn't there.

"That's okay," the kid's voice cracked. "Thank you for the sled." The kid smiled a smile so tight and forced it must have hurt.

"I tried telling you, kid, I'm not in the poodle finding business."

The kid nodded and opened his mouth the say something, but all that found its way out was a low mournful moan.

"That's enough, Mr. Caedwalla," the kid's mother snapped, taking her son into her arms. "It's a shame the cameras aren't here to film you breaking a little boy's heart."

Caedwalla ignored her comment. "Like I was saying, kid, I haven't got time to look for lost poodles, but I found an ugly mutt that needs a home." He motioned Rudolph to open the Escalade's door.

Bubbles bounded out of the SUV, practically knocking Rudolph over and leaped onto the kid, slobbering all over him. The kid screeched with a laughter, hugging the dog and holding on to it for dear life. The kid's mother sobbed watching their reunion. Even Rudolph sniffled.

"Thank you! Thank you! Thank you!" the kid shouted over Bubble's playful barking. "Thank you, Saint Nick!"

The kid's mother managed a nod of her head.

"You did good today, boss," Rodolph said. "Real good."

"You're both welcomed to join us for hot cocoa," the kid's mother offered.

Caedwalla dismissed the offer with a wave of his hand.

"Saint Nick likes bourbon. Neat," the kid pipped up. "Do we have bourbon?"

"Not at ten in the morning we don't," the kid's mother answered.

Caedwalla shrugged. "Then we'll be on our way."

"I imagine you're exhausted from delivering gifts and whatever else you been up to." She waited for an acknowledgment that never came. "According to the morning news, it was quite the night. The mayor's house was broken into. Every last gift was stolen, their Christmas stockings and the tree."

Rudolph shrugged.

"Also, an anonymous benefactor emptied every homeless shelter in the city," she continued, "and put the people up in a luxury hotel for the night, pampered them with haircuts, manicures, new clothes and a banquet fit for royalty."

"What a sap," Caedwalla said to Rudolph.

"And out of the blue I received a call from my parents. They purchased airline tickets for Chance and me to visit over Christmas vacation. If things go well, they'd like us to think about staying."

"Daryl's in jail," the kid told Caedwalla. "He robbed a bank."

"You don't say." Caedwalla looked incredulous.

"I don't know what you did," the kid's mother whispered, "but I doubt very much Daryl robbed a bank."

Caedwalla shrugged again "And yet his DNA was everywhere, witness after witness saw him, and there were videos and photographs of him. The guy was caught red-handed."

Rudolph chuckled.

"All Daryl remembers," the kid's mother explained, "was parking his truck that morning in the alley and then nothing else until the cops pulled him out his truck and put him in handcuffs. He doesn't deserve to jail for something he didn't do."

"Bubbles was beaten and starved when he was found chained to Daryl Clark's pickup. He deserves a lot more than jail time."

Rudolph nodded.

"My advice is to visit your parents, give the kid one of those genealogy DNA tests to maybe find his father. That kid deserves a dad. A good one."

"He does," the kid's mother agreed.

"Okay, Rudolph, time to get this sleigh on its way," Caedwalla said, climbing into the Escalade.

Caedwalla opened his window, waved a goodbye to the kid

and closed it promptly. "Call the hotel and extend my offer for another night's stay to everyone, including meals. And I feel like taking a ride this morning, Rudolph" He pulled the toy compass from his pocket and said, "Head north and let's see where it takes us."

December 25th is celebrated as Christmas Day.

AUTHOR BIOGRAPHIES

Ruth M. McCarty's short mysteries have appeared in Level Best Books anthologies, *Blunt Flash Trauma, Flash Bang Mysteries, Murder Most Edible* and *Over My Dead Body!* She won the 2009 Derringer Award given by the Short Mystery Fiction Society for her story "No Flowers for Stacey." She is a former editor at Level Best Books, a member of SinC and MWA and a founding member of New England Crime Bake.

Sharon Daynard's writing runs the gamut from light and quirky to downright dark and troubling. Her debut novel, *Murder Points North*, puts a humorous spin on murder in a small town. Her short stories include "The Boss of Butler Square" which received Honorable Mention for the Al Blanchard Award and "Widows Peak" which was short-listed for a Derringer Award. She's been offered the services of a hitman, crossed paths with a serial killer, testified before grand juries, and taken lie detector tests. She is a member of the New England chapter of Sisters in Crime.

Donna Ricci is a retired marketing writer who writes fiction as a great pleasure. She has written and edited a wide range of business documents and procedures, taught related seminars to colleagues and business partners and was Contributing Editor for a corporate news magazine distributed worldwide. Donna also copy edited a literary magazine and wrote many short stories and a couple of draft novels. She has been a member of the same writing group for more than twenty years. Donna lives in Massachusetts's Merrimack Valley. "Commencing Murder" is her first mystery short story.

Although most of her published writing is about the food and its travels, Carol Kaufman's favorite reading material has always been the mystery, ever since her long-ago first encounters with the Happy Hollisters and Nancy Drew. Since then, she has pored through (and lost sleep over) Agatha Christie, Louise Penny, P.D. James, and Ian Rankin, to name just a few. A few years ago, she decided to try her hand at fiction, so she joined Sisters in Crime to hone her skills.

When not collapsing under the weight of mounds of Japanese-to-English translation, Lauren Sheridan enjoys the classic mysteries of Agatha Christie, Louise Penny, and Anthony Horowitz. She developed an irrational fear while researching poisonous concoctions for her stories in this anthology that her Internet search history might put her on the FBI's most-wanted list. In addition to writing, Lauren enjoys photography and therapeutic watercolor painting. Her niece enjoys guessing what the paintings are. Lauren enjoys the 70% hit rate.

Randall DeWitt is the author of *Blunt Flash Trauma*, which includes stories by Ruth M. McCarty, Kathy Chencharik, and Sharon Daynard. His flash-fiction has appeared in *Alfred Hitchcock Mystery Magazine* with one of the stories, "The Cable Job," winning the 2012 Derringer Award for Best Flash Story. Other short mysteries by DeWitt have appeared in crime anthologies by Level Best Books and Untreed Reads.

Made in the USA
Middletown, DE
04 December 2021

53332001R00109